I0527032

THE EARL'S SCOTTISH HOYDEN

THE UPSTART CHRISTMAS BRIDES
BOOK FIVE

ALINA K. FIELD

HAVENLOCK PRESS

Copyright © 2023 Mary J. Kozlowski

ISBN No. 978-1-944063-48-1

Havenlock Press

PO Box 1891

La Mirada, CA 90637-1891

December 5, 2023

Cover Design by Dar Albert of Wicked Smart Designs

Edme Beecham was *not* disappointed in love last Christmas when Lord Cottingwith abruptly departed the Duke of Kinmarty's Yuletide party. No, the Earl was too old to be so shy, but there it was. He'd latched on to her own talkative self because he'd found Edme, a girl among a multitude of brothers of all ages, comfortable company. Thus, when an invitation to join a Yuletide party at Furningwood, his family's estate, arrives, she's alarmed to feel her hopes rising, and determined to stay home. But the earl is a valuable political and business connection, and her brother insists she go. After one youthful lapse, Trenton Yardley, Earl of Cottingwith, has set about being a better man than his late uncle and cousin, and restoring the fortunes of his family, without submitting himself to the sort of fortune-hunting marriage his mother wants for him. He has a secret, and only the right woman will do for him, one with a generous heart and a sense of humor. He'd thought he'd found her last year in

Edme Beecham, but an emergency had called him home before he could press his suit further.

The cold, aloof girl who appears at his home for Christmas could not be his Scottish hoyden, could she?

CHAPTER ONE

NOVEMBER 1823, EDINBURGH

"I won't do it, William." Edme Beecham punctuated the declaration with a pounding of her fist on the great walnut desk that had been her father's. "Send Archie on his own. I've no interest in the Earl of Cottingwith and no place in negotiating business with him."

Nor did Archie. Nor William for that matter, William who'd made an error in judgement just before Pa's death three years ago that nearly bankrupted Beecham trading. And for certain, the earl's interest was in doing business with them, not in courting Edme. His letters to William had made the first part clear, and anyone with an ounce of sense could read between the lines and judge the second to be true.

Besides, the business the earl was feeling around about was far too speculative, far too risky.

William's lips curved into an infuriating smile. "Ach. If I didn't know better, sister, I'd think ye were a lass spurned."

She tamped down her rising ire. "If ye're to send me away for Christmas again, I'd liefer travel to Kinmarty and visit Ann and Errol." She'd been a witness—she'd like to think a helpful one—to Ann and Errol's romance the year before. "She's increasing, you know."

"Ah, well, I'd expect Errol to get down to the business of—"

"*William.*"

He laughed. "Married to a doctor, Ann has no need of your services. And the duchess won't be there to entertain you. Kinmarty and his lady have traveled to London. Mrs. MacDonal is back from the Continent and planning to spend the Yuletide there."

"Well, aren't you well-informed?"

"Perhaps," he said, looking smug, "the Kinmartys will join you at Furningwood."

She shook her head. "No. Absolutely not."

"You don't wish to see the duke and his lady?"

She squeezed her eyes together in frustration. "Of course, I wish to see them. It's the notion that you think you're sending me off in quest of the earl's

2

hand that doesn't sit well. Especially since this proposal of his is…" She waved a hand. "We ought to limit ourselves to what we do best. Textiles. We don't know a thing about steam engines or shipbuilding."

In the months since she'd met the earl, he'd written many letters to her brother discussing business. He'd been down to Clydeside and visited ship works in Greenock. He wanted to involve the Beechams somehow, and she found… she didn't trust him. Not entirely. Not after the way he'd departed Kinmarty with his farewell conveyed by the duke.

"What does an English earl know about trade?" she asked. "He ought to confine himself to his crops and his livestock and squeezing rents out of his tenants."

William's feet hit the floor and he frowned. "Your heart was broken. Or was it something worse?"

"No." His lordship had been a gentleman, from his top hat to his polished boots. "Of course not. Has someone said that…" She took in a breath. Errol's letters to William she hadn't been able to find. She would box Errol's ears if he'd made such a report to her brother. "William, the earl was all that was gentlemanly and polite." And nothing more. "Had you been there and seen the others…" The marquess pursuing her cousin Ann had been plotting Ann's ruination if he couldn't obtain her hand and her dowry the respectable way. And he couldn't have, since Ann had been in love with Errol.

"I've not heard any aspersions regarding the earl's character," William said. "Only a comment from Errol that the man expressed an interest in learning more about Beecham Trading, which of course, I know from his correspondence. Errol hoped he might also have an interest in a match with ye."

"Well, he didn't, and he doesn't."

"Mayhap not. But if not, then why invite ye to his home?"

"He didn't invite me." She'd seen the letter from the Earl of Cottingwith. He'd invited the Beecham family. There'd been a reference to his earlier correspondence about his ship works and the wool and hops produced on the earl's estate. This was clearly an invitation extended to facilitate his business interests.

"Oh, aye, he did. Mentioned you by name."

"True. And you as well. Only because we are the only two Beechams he knows by name. 'Tis an invitation for business, William. Not wooing."

And that was how the party at Kinmarty the year before had been. The duke had called together a few noblemen to promote hunting on his lands. Her cousin, Ann, with her massive dowry, had been one of the lures, as well. Edme's invitation had been arranged by the duchess's cousin, Penelope

4

MacDonal, so that Ann was not the only young lady there.

Courting the heiress hadn't worked out as some of the cash-strapped guests had planned. Ann had spurned everyone except Errol—who wasn't truly a guest either, having been called to deliver his hostess's baby. Ann had forfeited her dowry for the chance to wed the man she'd loved since her girlhood.

"Well, then, sister. You've been helping with accounts, and inventory and correspondence for the past year, since we sent Peter off to Europe. I'm asking you to go along to this party for the sake of the Beecham family business."

"But I can't negotiate—"

"Archie will go with you."

"*Archie.*" Her nodcock brother had just turned eighteen. "And in point of fact, I know more about Beecham Trading—"

"Mayhap you do. That's why you'll be there, and mam too." William grinned. "No one expects you to sign contracts, Edme. Have a look at that ship works, and more importantly at the books. Archie will be able to take part in all the manly activities. With you and Mam there to rein him in, how much harm can he do?"

"I won't be there when he's out shooting or riding or visiting the nearest taproom." She plopped into the chair, thinking. Archie was a prodigious

5

flirt. She shot her brother a direct look. "And what about his proclivity for... wenching?"

He winced and grinned. "You heard? Nothing gets past you, does it, sister?"

Archie, tall, blond-haired, blue-eyed, and broad-shouldered, had been caught—almost caught—just before lifting the skirts of the daughter of one of the town burghers. The lass had set her cap for him, but rumor had it she was no innocent maid and knew well what she was about with a nincompoop like Edme's younger brother. Not that Archie was a total innocent. She didn't believe that for one moment.

"It's providential to remove him from town, don't you think? And besides, Rushton has asked me again about paying you court."

Lucas Rushton was one of the rising clerks in the business. His pursuit of Edme had subsided after she was sent off to Kinmarty the year before into the company of a duke, a marquess, an earl, and a baron's heir. As the months wore on and no noble engagement was announced, and no other invitations appeared, he'd quietly resumed sniffing around the barricades.

Despite his winking compliments, she knew he was chasing her for her dowry and a share in the family business, and she wouldn't have it.

All that would stop Rushton was either losing his position, which wouldn't help Beecham Trading, or sending Edme off for a time, as they'd done the year before. Perhaps William could throw him together with Archie's amorous lass.

"We'll need new gowns," she said, surrendering.

"There's a new shipment of fine cloth in the warehouse," he said. "Take what you need."

"An English earl's yuletide country house party," she mused. "The gowns must be the first stare of fashion." Unlike the ones she'd worn at Kinmarty last year, but that had been different. All the ladies there had been her friends.

"Fashionable. Of course," William said, "If you're to catch yourself an earl."

She grimaced. "Stop teasing. I was thinking more along the lines of showing off the prosperity of the family firm, brother."

Would that be the best tactic? Or, if Cottingwith was after a Beecham investment, would it be better to come looking like a frugal Scot?

Edme clenched her fists. She knew how these house parties worked. A single earl? There would be other young unmarried ladies attending, likely of higher status and greater wealth. Her dowry was respectable, but it wouldn't maintain a lord's grouse fields and stables.

She thought of the earl's attentions the previous year. She'd reviewed all the things he'd said, gone over them again and again, remembering the hard planes of his face and the way his lips hinted at a smile. He wasn't quite handsome, exactly, oh, not like Archie with his dazzling smiles and perfect features, but Cottingwith had charm of his own sort.

He'd been gentlemanly, and reserved, and very kind. And he'd shown no interest in marrying her.

Which was fine, wasn't it?

* * *

TRENTON YARDLEY, EARL OF COTTINGWITH, PUSHED his mount hard across the turned fields, clearing his mind of last night's argument, and the feverish dreams of red hair and amber eyes that had followed.

Somehow, Mother had sleuthed out or at least suspected his interest in Miss Edme Beecham, the young Scotswoman he'd met the year before. Mother's temper still flared when she thought of his absence from Furningwood the previous Christmas and the events that had followed. Among other things.

Blast it all, since the death of the late earl, his cousin, he'd worked every moment keeping Mother in the comfort his father had not been able to provide, God rest his father's soul, and his late uncle's as well.

His father had been a dreamer, a failed writer of poetry and just as dreadful a painter. The two previous earls, his uncle and cousin, had been

8

happy-go-lucky profligates, magnanimous in their hospitality, even when the bank account was empty.

It had been left to him to right the family ship.

Now the land was turning a profit. Sheep cropped the old earl's cricket field, the barley and hops yields had improved, and the brown weald cattle were fetching top prices in the London markets.

He was a bit of a dreamer as well, but a far more practical one. He'd spent his youth aboard ships and hadn't been able to shake the love of the sea. Now, the Yardley-Jelson Shipyard was on its way to being more than a notion, a fact he didn't share with Mother; she was horrified at the thought of her son the earl embracing a second ungentlemanly trade after the brickworks he'd founded.

Trade was risky, his mother believed. When a man had the extensive land holdings of an earl, why, riches grew yearly out of the soil. A business could fail in a heartbeat.

Thus, his invitation to the Beecham family had not gone over well. In fact, she'd categorically rejected the notion of inviting them when he broached the subject the night before.

She didn't know he'd sent the invitation himself weeks earlier, along with one to the Duke and Duchess of Kinmarty. If they accepted, Mother would have to simply put on a gracious demeanor and welcome them. And if not, the housekeeper would arrange rooms and hospitality. The butler—well, he would do as he was told, or find himself out of a job.

Though the duke had no money to invest, the duchess's cousin did, and they both had great influence with that lady. But that wasn't why he'd invited them. He knew that Edme would need their support.

Mother wouldn't mind the duke's and duchess's company. The Kinmartys were far from high in the instep, but Mother would forgive them their informality. When it came to titles, Mother was a terrible snob.

Edme Beecham was another matter. Ladylike she was, kind as well, with a sparkling beauty. If she was an Honorable or a Lady, mother might find her acceptable.

In fact, he'd gleaned from his conversations with her last year and the letters from William Beecham that Edme was *more* than just ladylike. She knew much about the family business. Might even be actively involved. Mother would have a snit, if she knew.

If the Beechams accepted. Neither they nor the Kinmartys had replied, unless Mother had waylaid the letters.

He supposed the letters ought to go to his mother, the current mistress of Furningwood. Not for much longer he hoped, and that thought brought a smile.

He turned his mount over to a groom and stalked into the breakfast room where the papers and several pieces of mail awaited him. While a footman poured coffee, Cottingwith filled a plate from a sideboard, took a seat and flipped through the mail.

Taylor, the butler, entered with more mail. "For Mrs. Yardley," he said, looking down his nose. "She's sent word that she'll be joining you for breakfast."

"Did she indeed?"

When Trent married, he might offer Taylor the chance to serve at the dower house with mother. Or he might boot him out of Kent entirely if his worst suspicions of the man proved to be true.

Mother usually breakfasted in her rooms. She'd likely be looking to pick up last night's argument. Cottingwith signaled. "I'll have a look."

He flipped through the letters, addressed in feminine handwriting to The Honorable Mrs. Mertice Yardley. It grated terribly on Mother that his father had died before getting the chance to make her a countess.

Kinmarty's lady might have directed a reply to his Yuletide invitation to his mother, but Beecham wouldn't have

He glanced through his own waiting stack and saw, with satisfaction, the healthy strong sprawl of

11

William Beecham, and the more elegant manly cursive of the Duke of Kinmarty.

His mother greeted him and gave a little laugh of pleasure at the pile of letters. "Replies to my invitations," she said. "At last. We will have you married before Shrove Tuesday, Cottingwith."

Though he was a fully grown man when he inherited, his own mother no longer called him by his Christian name.

He made a show of cutting his sausage. "In a hurry to move to the dower house, are you, Mother?"

She waved a hand. "That will come eventually, but I'll be needed here for a good long while as your bride settles into the role of countess."

"Oh? I thought most noble young ladies were schooled in running a household. Have you robbed the schoolrooms to bring me matrimonial candidates?" He'd reviewed the guest list himself with a view to which of the peers Mother sought might be interested in investment. He wasn't interested in their daughters.

She sent him a cautionary look and slid her gaze toward the footman pouring her tea.

Trent couldn't help chuckling. She could talk about having him married off, but he couldn't make a joke about the age of her intended bride.

Mother opened a letter and a smile bloomed on her lips. "The Darnleys will join us for Christmas along with their two daughters. I met them in London last season. Lovely girls. Very accomplished." She grimaced. "Their sons will come as well."

"Darnley's a good man," he said. *As well as wealthy with an active interest in trade.*

He cracked the seal on the duke's letter and read. They would come, the duke said, along with the ducal sprout. Kinmarty's heir had been born during last year's Yuletide party.

The duke was a fine fellow. Trent had met him in passing in London, when Kinmarty was plain Andrew MacDonal, before he'd inherited. The duchess was a sensible, pleasant woman who'd served for a brief time as the duke's housekeeper. Best not tell Mother that story.

Anticipation built in him as he picked up the second letter. He'd met Edme Beecham the previous Yuletide. He'd also had long talks with another guest, Dr. Errol Robillard, friend to the Beechams and their former employee. In the months since, he'd had regular correspondence with William Beecham, Edme's brother, head of the family and of the family firm.

The Beechams were important, and if they couldn't attend the house party, he would have to find a way to travel to Edinburgh after the New Year.

The seal cracked smoothly. He forced himself to

relax and nodded for his coffee cup to be refilled and then began to read.

William could not come. His wife would be entering her confinement and would, he said, have his guts for garters if he was away.

Despite his disappointment, he smiled. Theirs was not a marriage of convenience, it seemed.

"Oh." Mother fanned herself with her letter. "Good news. Lady Ottilia will attend. Such a pretty young thing, and the daughter and sister of a marquess. I've been corresponding with her aunt. I dared not to hope that she would accept the invitation. How marvelous."

He supposed he could dodge an extra single lady and her aunt for a few days. He nodded as the next lines of Beecham's letter caught his eye. If Cottingwith was agreeable, he would accept the earl's hospitality for his mother, Mrs. Beecham, and his younger brother, Archie, a very junior partner in the business. Edme would accompany them to keep Mrs. Beecham company and, William trusted, would acquit herself well in noble company. They were deputized to explore the business he wished to present but would not sign contracts. They would travel to London and join the Duke and Duchess of Kinmarty for the last leg of the journey.

The next paragraphs inquired about the state of his ship works. Trent folded the letter to read later in the privacy of his study.

"Three letters of regret," Mother moaned, buttering her toast. "But never mind, we shall have three young ladies staying with us, and then there will be several from the local families to attend our parties and balls, and if the weather is bad, some of them may wish to stay over." She looked up with a frown. "Are you sure we cannot extend the party until Twelfth Night? Sending them away on Boxing Day will give us less than a week."

House parties were costly. "You said you wished to offer ten dishes with every removal. Shall we adjust the menus and wine list? We have time to economize. And I'll be traveling to Chatham the week after Christmas, so you'll have to entertain without me."

He watched as she pressed her lips together with another cautionary side glance at the footman.

"Fine. These three young ladies, and three more from the village, and we'll have at least six marriageable young ladies of good family. You must make a choice, Cottingwith. It is high time you married and set up your nursery."

"Seven marriageable young ladies, mother."

She blinked.

"And one additional bachelor," he said. "Along with a married couple and their infant."

Color crept up her cheeks.

"You didn't. When I expressly said—"

"We must ready the nursery for the duke's heir."

She chuffed out a breath, eyes blinking, lips trembling and wavering between a smile and a frown. "The Kinmartys?"

"Yes. They will be bringing along Mrs. Beecham, and her children, Mr. Beecham and Miss Beecham."

"So many. We shall be squeezed... The duke and duchess... They are said to not be good ton, but nevertheless. Oh, but the others. Who are they? Perhaps the inn could accommodate—"

"Good heavens, mother. Wherever were you going to put those three who sent regrets? Put them in those rooms. Or put the bachelors together if you must. Have each married couple share a bedchamber." He waved a hand. "I trust that you and Mrs. Hunnycrest will work it out."

CHAPTER TWO

DECEMBER 20, 1823, FURNINGWOOD
MANOR, KENT

Edme Beecham held young Evan MacDonal, Marquess of Lithgow by his chubby hands as he stood on her lap, bouncing with each jolt of the carriage and crowing with delight.

"You won't laugh when he shoots milk onto your mantle." Andrew MacDonal, Duke of Kinmarty softened the statement with a smile and glanced out the window.

Milk on her mantle was the least of her worries, but despite her rising anxiety, she smiled and rubbed noses with the tiny marquess. Lucky lad. Confined to the nursery, he'd not have to face a houseful of elite strangers and one fickle earl.

"It won't be the first time, duke," she said. "If ye recall I have younger brothers as frisky as this wee lad."

As dusk fell, the coach lumbered off a rough country road between two pillars and onto a well-maintained private lane.

Filomena MacDonal, duchess of Kinmarty, lifted her head from her husband's shoulder. "Finally. A good road."

The buckskin clad leg of a rider appeared next to the coach. Archie Beecham peered down and rapped on the window. The duke dropped the glass.

"Furningwood." Archie grinned. "Can't see the house yet. Ye ought to come join me, duke. It's balmy as could be out here."

The duke shared a look with his wife, rapped on the roof, and opened the door. A cold breeze chilled them, but Archie was right, it wasn't as cold as the Beecham's home, Edinburgh, nor the Highlands where the duke and duchess made their home.

"Riding up top, John," the duke called. He chucked Evan on the cheek, dropped a kiss on the duchess's lips, and closed the door. The carriage swayed under his long legs until he settled, and they moved out.

"Andrew will be holding the lines," Filomena said. "He'll think it a great joke to arrive as the coachman." She smiled, slyly. "Cottingwith won't mind."

Ach, even the duchess was matchmaking. Edme

and her eldest brother, William, had nearly had a row over this Yuletide house party at the Earl of Cottingwith's home.

'Twas because of the Beecham family business that she'd surrendered to William's request that she attend, and she must swallow her pride and let her brothers and the duchess see they were all wrong about the earl's supposed interest in her own middle-class self.

Edme forced a chuckle. "He'll shock the servants."

Filomena shrugged and grinned.

"Do *you* not mind?" Edme asked.

"I'll only mind if he falls off and cracks his head. As for the servants, well, he is a duke, isn't he?"

'Twas simple for a duke and duchess to be easy about such a joke. For her own part, she was more discomposed now than she'd been last year arriving at the duke's Highland castle. A house party at a nobleman's house in England was a more fearsome thing. Especially the home of this nobleman.

She'd had many months to realize there was little warmth under his cold, dispassionate, English exterior. Her brother's open affection toward his wife, the duke's loving treatment of Filomena—Edme wouldn't settle for less than a man who would love her that way.

And she was sure her brother was wrong. This dreadful party wouldn't be about courtship.

At least she had a friend in the duchess. *And* her

nodcock of a brother, Archie. She'd also brought along Joanie, a housemaid she'd known all her life, to play lady's maid. Riding in the coach ahead of them with the duke's valet, the duchess's maid, and Evan's poor puking nurse, Morag, Joanie would have already arrived.

Filomena reached out her arms. "Shall I take back his nibs?"

Evan's eyelids drooped. Edme pulled him close and tucked his head to her shoulder. "Nay, I think not, Filomena." They'd been on a first name basis since last Christmas at Kinmarty Castle. "I'll spare the servants the shock of seeing a duchess carry her own child. We shan't tell them ye nurse him yourself else they'll chase us back to the carriage with their brooms."

Filomena's eyes crinkled in a smile and they both turned to the windows. Fat sheep dotted the grassy lawns, placidly grazing as the coach passed. When they turned at a bend, Archie called out to them to look.

Furningwood came into view.

"Oh my." Edme breathed out the words, butterflies stirring inside. In the descending dusk, torches illuminated the entrance and the festive green garlands draped over it.

Edme pressed her cheek to the window. "'Tis as large as Castle Kinmarty."

"Larger, I'd wager," Filomena said. "There'll be wings."

"But it's not nearly as old."

"No. I'd guess it was built perhaps a hundred years ago during the time of Queen Anne. And the red brick is local. We shall ask Cottingwith. Andrew said he has brick works along with a great number of investments and plans."

A great number. And some plans that involved Beecham Trading, which was the only reason she'd agreed to this journey. But her brothers would not be buying and selling bricks, nor building ships if she could help it.

Wool though... She glanced out the window. She was a city girl. She knew her wool but not her sheep. Perhaps Cottingwith was raising a certain breed and besides his ship works' venture, also hoped to have the Beechams trade the cloth made from it.

When the carriage stopped, several people appeared, a stiff old poker in black and younger men in bright red livery. Grooms gathered at the horses' heads, but her vision filled with the sight of one man, dressed like her brother in buckskins and a cutaway coat. He was hatless, and his brown hair ruffled in the sharp breeze. A surprised smile lit his face when he recognized the duke jumping down from the coachman's perch.

His gaze slid to the coach and Edme pressed back

against the squab until Archie's approach to their host blocked the view.

A footman opened the coach door.

"After ye, your grace," Edme said, wrapping her shawl around Evan's head. "Ye must make a grand appearance."

Filomena laughed and accepted the footman's hand.

Edme held the sleeping babe securely and climbed out. The day was advanced, the sky cloudy, and the chill wind sliced through the air carrying with it the scent of horses and grass.

"Miss Beecham." The Earl of Cottingwith appeared in front of her. He dipped his head and gave her one of his reserved smiles, making her heart thump and her mouth go dry. The cold air had ruddied his cheeks under his afternoon beard. He was as braw and handsome as ever and seemed not a bit jumpy to see a woman he'd jilted a year before.

No. He hadn't jilted her. There'd been no promises made, not even any talk of them.

"Who have you there?" he asked.

"Shh," she said. "This is Lord Lithgow. I've the honor of carrying in a marquess."

"Your grace. Welcome." A stout older lady had joined them and was curtsying low to Filomena and Kinmarty. She glanced toward Edme and signaled a servant. "Mrs. Hunnycrest will have someone show your nursemaid upstairs."

Filomena's lips were twitching, and she herself wanted to laugh.

Cottingwith's cheeks turned a deeper shade of red. The surprise press of his hand on Edme's back sent a tingle through her. He steered her toward the older lady. "Mother, meet one of our guests, Miss Edme Beecham. Miss Beecham, my mother, Mrs. Mertice Yardley."

Edme swallowed a wry smile at the lady's haughty frown and managed a small curtsy.

"And the sleeping one is Lithgow," Filomena whispered, taking her son from Edme. She went on in a low voice. "I beg your pardon, Mrs. Yardley, but he'll be hungry again soon. I should like to visit my room before conveying him to the nursery."

Cottingwith's mother's eyebrows rose, but she said "of course," and a maid led Filomena and the sleeping babe away.

Archie had apparently already been introduced, and he fell into step beside Edme as Cottingwith ushered them into the hall where servants took their wraps. 'Twas the housekeeper herself, a thin lady with sharp features, who led Edme off to her assigned bedchamber. Like Lot's wife, Edme couldn't help a glance back at their host, and she caught the nod he exchanged with his housekeeper.

A shiver went through her. What did it mean?

* * *

BEFORE TRENT COULD ENJOY HIS GUESTS, HIS DUTIES as an earl got in the way.

"I just had a message from Davis. They're awaiting a hoy that was supposed to leave Calais a day ago," said Sir Henry Rylston.

Sir Henry, local justice of the peace, had sent word to Trent asking for this hasty clandestine meeting at the boundary of their two estates. A middle-aged man who'd spent a great deal of time in diplomatic posts on the continent, he'd returned to his estate after his wife's death. Their joint efforts to curb smuggling had led to a close friendship.

"Their informant mentioned one of your men as the contact," Sir Henry said, "but didn't have a name."

Trent grimaced, his mood suddenly as gloomy as the descending night. For the last several months he'd been working closely with Sir Henry and Captain Jared Davis, the local Riding Officer. They had rendered the cottage that had been the gang's usual storage place unusable, but that hadn't stopped the free trading. Nor had the prosecution and transportation of one of Trent's tenants several months ago.

"Do you still believe it's Taylor?" Sir Henry asked.

Taylor was the butler Trent had inherited along with the title, a longtime resident of Kent with deep ties to the community.

"I've no evidence," he said, "but also no doubt."

What he wasn't certain of was his mother's

involvement, and that had given him pause to proceed carefully. Mother valued expensive goods any way she could get them. Taylor had played on her greed from their very first meeting.

"I know your worries," Sir Henry said. They'd discussed this before. "I'm sworn to uphold the law, but I'm not averse to seeing a blackguard keelhauled instead of prosecuted before sullying a friend's mother's reputation."

Even if she deserves it?

He shook off the thought. He had the means and the contacts to see Taylor privately transported. He'd send an express to his business partner, Thomas Jelson.

He was, however, not yet ready to give up on his mother. Though her treatment of Edme Beecham might be the last straw he allowed to poke him.

Edme, with her sparkling hair, her sweet disposition, and her good sense. When she'd alighted from the carriage framed by the torchlight with Kinmarty's child, he pictured her glowing, carrying his child—his and hers—in her arms. The long months since he'd seen her had been filled with attention to duty, patient self-restraint, careful planning, and now it would all be worth it, he prayed.

"I'll send a note when I hear more. Meanwhile, I've accepted your mother's invitation to dinner two night's hence."

"Excellent. Mother is planning seventeen courses. She'll be in alt to have the justice of the peace in attendance."

He hoped.

Sir Henry chuckled. "If that's so, it will be a good sign and should soothe your worries."

Sir Henry bid him farewell and picked his way into the darkness.

Trent turned his horse toward home, passing the cottage on the edge of the orchard. He'd paid a call on the occupants before meeting Sir Henry. The former warehouse for the gang, the cottage had been refurbished inside and out. As he passed, lamplight shone through the window and smoke wafted from the chimney.

All was well there. In any case, there wasn't time now to stop. He'd need to shave and prepare for his dinner guests and the chance to see Edme again.

"THE NURSEMAID, MOTHER?" HE MURMURED, escorting her to the parlor where all the guests would gather shortly. They hadn't had a chance for a private conversation earlier before his quick meeting with Sir Henry.

"How was I to know?" She shrugged. "Her grace didn't seem to mind."

Nor had Edme seemed flustered. In fact, a smile

had been lurking on her lips, as if the two ladies had pulled a joke on their hostess.

"The brother is a handsome one. You must watch that he doesn't steal a march on you with the young ladies. Though he's very young." She made a face. "And in trade."

He looked forward to knowing Archie better. Furningwood had a bailiff to manage the farms and the livestock, but in the last year he'd lost his secretary. He needed a new man, someone with a head for business. Someone he could trust. Hiring Archie might strengthen his ties with the Beecham family.

There was another tie he intended to pursue, and it might be an uphill battle. Though Edme had seemed amused at Mother's faux pas, he'd sensed a coolness about his Scottish hoyden.

Rightly so, and he itched for the chance to explain to her, for in the last year he'd realized that, besides wanting her, he needed her. She was the one person, he suspected, who could help him put things right.

Mother had spoken several times of her matchmaking plans for this house party, but he had some of his own.

"I'm glad Mrs. Beecham wasn't able to attend," mother said. "Else we would have been out of balance with our ladies and gentlemen."

"And how terrible that would be," he teased.

At the last moment, Edme's mother had decided to stay in Scotland. In truth, he was glad as well. The duchess was more likely to be a lax chaperone for Edme.

"Where did you go earlier, Cottingwith?" Mother asked.

He turned a sharp gaze on her. He wouldn't tell her of the meeting with Sir Henry. "Where I go every day."

"You ought to send them away for the Yuletide."

He walked to the window and looked out on the lawns. There, beyond the old cricket fields and the thick elms, smoke puffed from the chimney of the small red brick cottage.

"You must tell Mrs. Ewell to keep her inside and away from our guests," Mother said.

He glanced back to see red creeping up her cheeks. "I'll do no such thing, and you've no right to ask it of me. Your color is rising—do you plan to go into a rage now? That would not serve either of our interests, would it?"

It might discourage the young ladies on her list of potential brides and their parents, but his mother's explosive disposition might also drive away Edme.

"The guests will gather for dinner soon," he added calmly, quietly, just the way his last captain would do when an enemy ship hove into view. He'd learned much from that honorable commander about curbing his temper and conducting himself as a man. He hadn't entirely tamed all his wild hares, the consequences of which had been schooling him for the last twelvemonth.

Footsteps resounded outside the parlor, growing louder, and he turned back to the window. It was too late to talk further with mother. Too late as well for her protests and demands. He'd paid a visit that morning and issued an invitation.

Not all the festivities would be suitable for a child, but some would be, and he'd told Mrs. Ewell to bring Sally around for them. The girl's eyes had lit up under her usual scowl. He'd told Sally she must be on her best behavior, and she'd said, grudgingly, yes uncle, I promise.

Sally Brown, the girl who called him uncle. Not his niece at all.

LORD DARNLEY CALLED A GREETING, AND TRENT turned back to his duties as host of the party. Mother had put on her Lady of the Manor face and was welcoming Lady Darnley and her two daughters, Diana, the elder of the two, and Helen. The Darnley sons followed behind. The elder, Hector, had just taken up one of his father's seats in the Commons and had not yet fallen into the idle life of a town dandy. But he would, Trent suspected. The other, Simon, had not yet reached his majority.

The arrival of the duke and duchess evoked deep curtsies and nervous chatter from the younger ladies, until Archie and Edme entered.

The Darnley offspring all grew wide-eyed at the sight of the fair-haired young man and the sparkling redhead. For his part, he had no qualms about losing the romantic interest of the young ladies. But when Hector and Simon stepped forward to speak with Edme, he had to employ all of his willpower to hold himself back.

"From Scotland, are they?" Lord Darnley asked. Trent hadn't noticed him moving up next to him.

"Edinburgh," Trent said. "Miss Beecham is an acquaintance of the Kinmartys."

"Landed?"

"The family owns a trading company."

"Hmm. Good dowry?" Despite his title, Darnley had several business interests, one reason why Trent had approved of his appearance on the guest list.

When he didn't answer, Darnley shrugged. "Bit abrupt, I know, but Hector seems interested, and my lady will be trying to ferret it out of someone."

"I actually don't know."

He didn't know the exact amount, but last Christmas at the duke's party, Edme's cousin had worried that the fortune hunter futilely pursuing *her* might turn to Edme for her respectable dowry.

What was respectable always depended on the fortune hunter's needs. The cash-strapped Marquess of Hatherton had plagued the Kinmarty party last Christmas with his greed. If Edme's dowry was enough to tempt that bounder, it would be more than enough for an earl getting his estate and businesses sorted out.

The truth was, he'd take Edme with no dowry. She fairly glowed in a bronze silky gown that showed her red hair and sparkling amber eyes to advantage. His goddess.

When she looked up at the elder Darnley boy and accepted a sherry from him, jealousy swept over Trent in a hot angry avalanche. Of their own accord, his feet carried him toward her.

EDME ACCEPTED THE GLASS FROM COTTINGWITH'S guest—what was his name? Henry? No—Hector— and felt her nerves easing. Hector was of an age with her brother, Peter, and the other Darnley lad couldn't be any older than Archie and was probably just as much a nodcock. She felt very much at home with giddy male nodcocks. Even the older men, like her brother William or the duke—both were silly enough to put her at her ease. It was the serious sort of man—like Cottingwith, that made her nervous.

Though last year, she'd finally begun to feel comfortable in his company. Just before he left without explanation.

"Edinburgh?" Hector said. "I've always wanted to go there."

"Does your family reside in town?" the younger one asked.

While she chatted with them, she watched Cottingwith approaching and inwardly shook herself. She was here representing Beecham Trading. Celebrating an English Christmas was a rare treat. She would enjoy herself, yes she would, but she—and Archie, if he wasn't too distracted by the young ladies—would find out just what the Earl of Cottingwith wanted from their family business.

Cottingwith joined them and she made a respectable curtsy.

"I had no chance to ask earlier, Miss Beecham," he said, with his usual soberness, "but I trust your journey was a pleasant one?"

"Pleasant enough. The weather was fair, and we were able to abide a few days in London before traveling on." She took a sip. "Ye've a very, er, grand home here, my lord."

Drat, she ought to be able to come up with a better rejoinder than that, but her nerves were jangling again.

When he asked about her mother and William, and then wanted to know how her cousin Ann and Ann's new husband Errol Robillard were faring, her nerves eased. Ann and Errol had married last Christmas after a brief rocky courtship.

From a distance, she saw Filomena lean close to her husband, and then the duke called across the room to Hector and Simon to come join him.

Filomena smiled, shrugged, and turned the full force of her attention on Cottingwith's mother and the elder Darnleys.

Irritation made Edme's cheeks prickle, and she wondered if her color was rising. A glance at Cottingwith revealed a smug look of satisfaction.

"And now, ye have me alone, sir," she said.

His lips quirked and more heat flared in her. She was flirting, against her better judgment.

"Shall I call my brother over to join us? He knows we're here to discuss trade, but I fear he can't help but draw the attention of the lasses."

"Miss Edme Beecham, I hope you're not here just for business. I should like you to enjoy Christmas here at Furningwood Manor with me. And I'm grateful to Archie for drawing the attention of all the other young ladies." His gaze warmed her, and a smile curved his lips. "As long as he doesn't draw his sister's attention away from me."

A shiver chased the heat down her spine into her nether regions. Thank heavens the lavish Yuletide decorations didn't include kissing balls.

She held his gaze, determined that she wouldn't look away.

A year ago, she'd denied any tendre for him, but that had been her pride speaking, and her hurt feelings, and best she remember the ache his sudden departure had caused her. Best they get on with whatever business he wanted to conduct. And best she avoid these intimate moments.

He'd left her disappointed a year ago—there, she'd admitted it to herself. He seemed a good enough man, or so William thought. But how could she ever trust him with her heart?

What was she to do?

She forced a smile. "I'm here to represent Beecham Trading. And also to keep Archie out of trouble." She nodded toward her brother, who had both of the Darnley girls giggling.

Cottingwith chuckled and opened his mouth to speak, but the door opened, and he turned that way, and his whole demeanor transformed. His mouth tightened and his eyes widened and flashed and then settled into a hooded gaze.

Edme followed his line of sight and her skin prickled and crawled. "Hatherot," she said through clenched teeth.

CHAPTER THREE

The Marquess of Hatherot was as handsome a blond Adonis as Archie, if one discounted the weathering from fifteen additional years of hard living and his general aura of dissipation. He'd arrived with a handsome lady who had a smudge of mud on her skirts.

Cottingwith uttered a low curse and set a hand to her back, his touch easing her.

"Lady Ottilia." Mrs. Yardley hurried over to greet the new arrivals.

"Has he married then?" Edme asked. She wouldn't have to run quite as hard from the wretch if Hatherot had found himself a fat purse.

"I fear that's his sister." He offered his arm, his countenance grim. "Mother mentioned a Lady Ottilia attending. I ought to have remembered he's her brother. Will you come with me to greet them?"

Come with him? And what message was that supposed to send to Hatherot and everyone gathered there?

Cottingwith raised an eyebrow, waiting.

She glanced at Hatherot who had a predatory gleam in his eye, and then back to Cottingwith. He'd assumed a mask, but she could see the determination lurking in his gaze.

Last year at Kinmarty, Cottingwith had provided Edme protection from the predatory marquess, and he was doing the same now. But at what price this time?

No, she'd find a way to protect herself from Hatherot while guarding her heart from her host.

Hatherot turned to speak to the dark-haired lady who was his sister. She shared her blond-haired brother's square jaw and jutting chin, yet her face was more sculpted, the angles harder, the planes hollower, as if she'd been ill. Like her brother, her shoulders were broad and squared off over a tall straight-up-and down shape that was more wiry than willowy. When she glanced their way, her eyes seemed to hold the same predatory gleam as her brother's.

She was seeking a fat purse also, and she had Cottingwith in her sights.

Edme reached for his arm and said, "Aye. I will."

* * *

TRENT TOUCHED EDME'S HAND AND STEELED HIMSELF. The Marquess of Hatherot, one of the greatest pieces of slime in all of Great Britain, stood in his parlor and Mother was gushing greetings.

Lady Ottilia. The name had nagged at his memory when Mother mentioned her as a guest, but he'd been so consumed with thoughts of the lady on his arm that he hadn't delved deeper.

He knew of Hatherot's sister. He'd seen her at social events, but they'd never been introduced, nor had he ever claimed an introduction. In the men's clubs, she was probably the most whispered about young woman of the ton. Young being a relative term, because at her age—something like five and twenty—she would be considered on the shelf by many.

There'd been nibbles on her matrimonial hook, but despite her beauty, no one had taken the bait fully. Beauty was a wonderful thing, but most men of good character were looking for a woman of similar character, and if she brought a dowry, so much the better. Lady Ottilia was endowed with the first but was said to be lacking the last two. Whatever dowry the last marquess had arranged for her had been gambled away by the current incumbent.

She was also rumored to have had affairs, to have gone away for several months. A mercury treatment or childbirth? The gadabouts at the clubs whispered behind their hands, though no one had inscribed the

37

speculation into the betting book lest they be called out by her brother.

Trent listened to gossip, of course, because anything might affect his business. A loss of reputation might mean a loss of influence in Parliament and a political failure affecting contracts and private bills. He *listened* to gossip, but he had a firm rule about spreading it—*people who live in glass houses shouldn't throw stones.* In any case, Lady Ottilia was not part of his circle, nor would she ever be.

Yet here she was. Where on earth had his hotheaded, social-climbing mother encountered the woman?

He hadn't spoken to Hatherot since last Christmas at Kinmarty. There were rumors of ore deposits on one of his entailed properties, and the possibility of building a foundry on the estate. Perhaps he was here to float shares for whatever wild-eyed gambler would be willing to take a risk on the Marquess of Hatherot's business acumen.

He'd also still be shopping for a dowry for himself, and a prize for his sister.

Trent had two more reasons to keep Edme Beecham close this week, his own protection as well as hers.

"My lord, Lady Ottilia," Mother said, "may I introduce my son, Cottingwith?"

"Hatherot and I are already acquainted," he said. "Lady Ottilia, may I present Miss Edme

Beecham? Miss Beecham, I'm sure you remember Hatherot from the Kinmarty's Yuletide party last year."

Hatherot's lips twitched. "A pleasure to see you again, Miss Beecham."

Edme gave the smallest of curtsies.

"Have you only just arrived?" Mother asked. "I hope your journey was pleasant."

"Terrible roads until we reached your excellent lane," Hatherot said.

"How festive your home is. May we freshen up and join you at dinner? We shall be quick about it." Lady Ottilia's voice was a practiced slither that nevertheless chafed across his skin.

"Of course." Mother signaled a footman. "We'll let Cook know. Do join us as soon as you're able."

A duke, a marquess, and a baron at her Christmas celebration. Mother was in alt as she ushered away the two newest guests and hurried to send word to the kitchens.

"Surprised you invited Hatherot." The duke had appeared on Edme's other side.

"I didn't," Trent snapped.

Edme's hand slipped away. "Then why is he here?"

He shook his head. "I fear Mother added their names to the guest list on the sly. But that is, I suppose, ungracious of me to say."

"He was a surprise guest at our house party last

Christmas as well." The duchess had joined them. "Who was that woman with him?"

"His sister."

She wrinkled her nose. "I was looking forward to an easy time of chaperoning you, Edme," she said. "But I see I shall have to be very attentive. And you, Andrew, I expect I'll have to look out for you as well."

The duke laughed heartily. "She doesn't hold a candle to you, my love. It's the single young gentlemen we must worry about."

Trent felt all eyes on him. "No." He shook his head. "I'm not interested."

"Oh ho," the duke said. "How unchivalrous."

Trent caught Edme's eye and smiled. "Chivalry requires the right partner."

The duke was determined to goad him. "But attempts to entrap..."

"Won't work."

"Nevertheless," the duke said, "I shall be your constant companion."

"Your grace," Edme said. "I'd be eternally grateful if ye'd extend your protection to my nodcock of a brother."

He exchanged a look with the duke. Trent didn't spread gossip as a rule. Archie wouldn't very likely have heard the club gossip, but if he had, perhaps, at his age, he'd find it more enticing than off-putting.

"Don't worry, Edme," the duchess said. "Andrew

will look after Archie as well. Now, let me steal you away to mingle with the Darnley lasses."

He caught a hint of warning in her grace's tone—he'd given Edme enough attention to stir talk. Fair enough.

"I trust you're still an early riser, Miss Beecham," he said. "There are a few pleasant walks in the Furningwood gardens, even at this time of year."

She blinked and tilted her head in a questioning manner, and then nodded. "And I should love to see them."

He watched her depart, mesmerized by the sway of her hips under the bronze silk.

"I say, Cottingwith." Archie Beecham had joined Kinmarty and both men were eyeing him. "Perhaps ye and I ought to talk about more than your ship works."

Kinmarty chuckled and walked away.

Trent glanced back at Edme. His mother was advancing from the other side of the room, and he saw that Hatherot and his sister had indeed only freshened up, not changed altogether. In a moment, the dinner gong would sound. Hatherot made a beeline for Edme and touched her arm to turn her to face him.

He sensed Archie bristling next to him and saw the lad's face darken.

"Beecham, can we speak tonight?" Trent asked. "Perhaps after the ladies retire."

. . .

THAT NIGHT, JOANIE HELPED EDME INTO HER nightgown and robe, and plaited her hair, all the while strangely mum. A Scotswoman of the big-boned, well-fed variety, Joanie wasn't a chatterbox or a complainer, but neither was she a timid mouse. Quite the opposite, in fact.

"What's bothering ye?" Edme asked. "How were matters below stairs?"

"I ken that there's summat amiss. What, I'm not certain yet. Need to sort the earl's servants from the visitors' folks. Supper was good and plenty."

Joanie frowned into the mirror. "This suite, though, Miss Edme. Fit for the king, if I do say so."

She'd had the same thought when she arrived that afternoon. The green suite, the housekeeper had called it, had a generous-sized sitting room; a bedchamber with more chairs, a sofa, and a wide tester bed; and a side room for clothing with a cot for the maid.

"The earl wants a deal with Beecham trading," Edme said.

"*Hmph.* As long as that's all he wants."

The sound of a door clicking shut filtered in from the sitting room.

"More hot bricks? Hold this." Joanie handed the end of the unfinished plait to Edme and strode to the door.

Edme heard her loud gasp and followed, peering around the maid.

Cottingwith held a position in the middle of the room, arms crossed.

"Milord," Joanie growled, and would have said more, but Edme grasped the lapels of her robe with one hand and her plait with the other and pushed the maid aside.

"Have ye lost your way to your bedchamber, milord?" she asked.

Some of the tension went out of him. "I've come to talk. Your brother will be along in a few minutes, but I wanted to speak to you first." He slid a glance at Joanie. "Alone, if you please."

"Archie is coming?"

"Yes."

"Joanie, wait in the bedchamber. Ye may keep the door open. I'll call for ye if the earl gives me cause."

His face broke into a smile that took her breath away. "I won't, Joanie." He extended his hand and shivering, she dropped her plait and let him take her hand, leading her close to the windows, away from both the door to her bedchamber and the door to the corridor.

His gaze swept over her. If she didn't know she was still perfectly covered from her neck to her bare toes, she'd swear she'd just been undressed.

His gaze lingered awhile on her feet and when he

raised his eyes to her, they fair glowed with a heat that sent ripples through her.

He touched the plait that hung over her breast down to her waist. "This glorious hair. I wondered how long it was."

She summoned some sauciness. "And n-now ye know." Hades, her voice had trembled.

Cottingwith's gaze strayed to her breasts again, and she wondered if the white dressing gown and the nightgown underneath quite concealed her. The light from the branch of candles on the mantel lit sparks in his eyes.

He moved his hands down to envelope hers, and she found herself shivering, wishing he would pull her into his arms and warm her, waiting for it.

She must get a grip on herself.

"I didn't want to wait to speak to you. I owe you the truth, don't I, Edme? The truth, an apology, and an explanation for why I left Kinmarty so suddenly last Christmas."

Her breath caught and she raised her eyebrows, summoning her pride. "Ye made no promises—of course ye don't—"

"I do owe you." He set a finger to her lips, and she wished it were his lips touching hers instead.

A kiss. Just a kiss.

"Given the attention I showed you, you had every right to expect more from me last Christmas. I wasn't forthright with you, but I *was* courting you.

44

Had matters progressed as I'd hoped, I would have traveled to Edinburgh and met your mother and brothers. I would have invited all of you south so you might know me better before deciding. It was what I meant to do. I *was* courting you, *am* courting you now, if you'll allow it."

That distracting finger sketched a line along her cheek to just below her ear.

He was courting her, but he hadn't said anything because he wanted to meet her mother and brothers, and… "Is that why ye started writing to William? Were ye asking his permission to court me? Or…" She wrinkled her nose. "Are ye planning to seek Archie's?"

"I'm asking you first."

His hand cradled her jaw and slid round to cup the back of her head.

That had been the right answer. She sighed, leaned forward, and her lips finally met his.

The sound of the latch turning had her jumping away, though Cottingwith still held onto her hand.

"Here now," Archie said. "What are ye aboot?"

"Yes?" Cottingwith murmured for her ears only. "May I court you?

Her breath came in short gasps, and she fought to control it. He'd hurt her before. She couldn't entirely trust him.

Oh, but she wanted to.

"Yes?" Cottingwith prompted.

"Courtship, aye," she whispered. "No other promises. And this doesna involve Archie."

He nodded and led her to the sofa. "Archie, come join us. I want to tell you a bit about our plans for the ship works."

Cottingwith didn't stay long, nor did he go into many details about his business partner, Jelson, yet as he touched on steam engines, steel hulls and tonnage, she stifled a yawn, and then realized as soon as he and Archie departed, he'd never told her why he'd left Kinmarty so suddenly.

That was a question that must be answered before any courtship would get underway.

AFTER A RESTLESS NIGHT OF TOSSING AND TURNING, Edme finally shoved off the covers at the first sign of dawn and leapfrogged from carpet to carpet to the hearth where she stirred the embers, shoveled in fresh coal, and rubbed her hands over the rising heat. A gown and underthings had been laid out for her the night before, and she hurried to don the fresh chemise.

The dressing room door creaked. "I was just about to wake ye, miss," Joanie said with a yawn.

"Ach," Edme said, "thank ye, Joanie. As it happens, I couldna sleep." Strange, because the talk of shipbuilding had nearly had her dozing. "If ye but help me with these fastenings and my hair ye can hie back to your bed for another hour."

"I'm dressed and if ye're to walk, I must—"

"No, no, the sun will be up soon and the kitchen staff stirring. There'll be no harm to me walking alone."

Besides, she wouldn't be alone, at least not unless she'd misunderstood Cottingwith's comment about being an earlier riser, an implied invitation if ever she'd heard one.

A part of her hoped she'd misunderstood, and that they wouldn't continue the conversation about courtship this morning, or ever. It would be far, far easier to get through this Yuletide house party, if her only interactions with Cottingwith concerned business. If matters of the heart were not in play. And if he didn't show up, well, she'd know, wouldn't she? She would see that he truly wasn't a man she could trust.

It took some doing, but she persuaded her new lady's maid back to the small cot that held a mattress almost as thick as her own.

She looked around her beautifully appointed bedchamber with its cherrywood bed and bureau, and curtains in a cheery spring green.

Had Cottingwith truly arranged it especially for her?

It was luxurious, and to be sure, she was glad not

to share with guests who were strangers. The Darnley boys were together in a chamber on this floor, and the Darnley girls in another along the same passage. Archie had a small closet of a room across the hall. The married couples and the marquess and his sister had been placed elsewhere, in another wing, and happy she was not to have the marquess wandering along the passage near her bedchamber.

She tied the laces of her stout half boots and went to the window, opening it a crack. Morning fog obscured the sun, but the gray light had brightened, and there was no bite in the air's chilliness. She pulled on the pelisse she'd worn in the carriage. The pocket still held a clean handkerchief and the few squares of shortbread she'd brought along to settle her stomach.

She was, she realized, hungry, and breakfast would come later. If Cottingwith didn't appear she'd find a bench somewhere and eat them.

She pulled on her gloves and shawl and stepped quietly into the passage.

Nerves jangling, she kept to the long carpet runner, her steps silent. Whispering a good morning to a tweenie carrying a bucket of coals, Edme made her way down the carpeted stairs to the hall. A figure stepped out from the shadows, startling her.

"You're awake." Cottingwith reached for her hand and bowed over it. He was dressed in buckskins and boots, with a green waistcoat and black coat, and he smelled of shaving soap and leather polish. His dark hair was overlong and badly combed, a lock hanging over his forehead begging her hand to brush it back.

She clutched her hands at her waist.

"Will you be warm enough?"

"Aye." She nodded, suddenly breathless.

He pried one of her hands free and enfolded it in his much larger one. "Come this way."

They passed down a back corridor to a carved wooden door. He unlocked it, and ushered her in. "My study," he said.

A lamp burned dimly on a massive desk near a pile of letters, as if he'd already been working and had just turned the wick lower.

"Sometime today, I'd like to show you and Archie the plans we discussed last night. We'll have privacy here." Still holding her hand, he tugged her along to a French window. "We'll just pop out to the terrace here and avoid disturbing the staff."

Sneaking out together unobserved. She ought to be nervous, but she was only intrigued. Stimulated. *Oh Hades.*

He closed the door and locked it. "We're applying for a patent. No sense in tempting prying eyes."

Like those of the Marquess of Hatherot.

They passed down a set of shallow steps onto a flagstone path bordered by a boxwood hedge that shielded them from the house.

Then he tugged her closer, making her shiver. "Still warm enough?"

She inwardly shook herself. "Should I get any warmer I'll have to slap ye, my lord."

He sent her a shocked look and eased his grip. And then he smiled. "It's forewarned, I am," he said in a mock Scots accent.

Laughing, she looked around. On this side of the hedge, a sweeping lawn ended at what she would guess was an orchard. "Are those apple trees?"

"Yes, and cherry trees as well. On the other side of the hedge is a knot garden and a small maze. We have a rose garden nearer the house. You must see everything in summer. The gardens were my great-uncle's doing, and they were in quite a state when I inherited. I've been able to hire enough workers to bring the gardens around, and also to keep starvation at bay for some of our local families."

Starvation had haunted post war England and Scotland. It was a mark in his favor that he'd seen fit to do his small part.

"Furningwood has a good enough income to be self-sustaining?"

He glanced down, smiling. "Is that Miss Edme Beecham of Beecham Trading asking?"

The question, the teasing tone, startled her and stirred her temper. "Is it an impertinent question for aristocratic company like yours?"

His gaze locked her in place, the warmth in his

eyes stirring what she could now see were flecks of the deepest forest green in the irises. Hazel eyes, not true brown, and in an unusual pattern of color. The corners of his eyes crinkled, still holding the smile.

"An investor might ask it," he said. "Or… a father or brother receiving a request for a lady's hand."

Rendered speechless for a moment, she found her breath and nodded. "I see. Or the question may simply come from an ignorant uncouth Scotswoman."

His smile fell away. "No." He lifted her hand and pressed a kiss to it. "Forgive me for teasing you. It's a fair question from a lady I'm courting. And yes, at the present, Furningwood is self-supporting, though I must tell you we are not living in quite the luxury of many titled houses."

Though they'd talked of it the night before, her heart still stuttered over the words, *a lady I'm courting,* and it took a moment for her mind to catch up with the rest of what he'd said.

She thought of the sumptuous dinner the night before, and she was speechless again. If that wasn't luxury, what was?

"Last Yuletide at Kinmarty…" He pressed his lips together and his brow furrowed.

Yes, this was the reason she'd come out for this walk. She needed to know why he'd left without a farewell. "You were called away."

"Yes. I must explain—"

"Uncle." The cry came from a child's voice, accompanied by sharp barks growing louder. Cottingwith whipped around and stooped to receive a young girl who barreled into his arms while a wiry-haired terrier bounced at their feet.

CHAPTER FOUR

The girl pulled away, waving a note in Cottingwith's face. "Look, uncle. A note from Father Christmas."

"Indeed." Cottingwith took the scrap of paper, scanned it, and stuffed it into his pocket. "Now, Sally Brown, let us remember our manners."

He turned the little lass to face Edme, and the girl looked up, a frown creasing the pale face under a knitted cap. Tangled brown hair streamed from under the cap's ribbing and spilled over a warm woolen cloak.

"Miss Beecham," he said, "may I make known to you my ward, Miss Sally Brown? Sally," he said, coaxingly.

The girl executed a clumsy curtsy, and then hesitantly extended her ungloved hand to allow Edme to shake it. The little hand was cold as ice.

"It's pleased, I am, to make your acquaintance, Miss Sally," Edme said, and then her breath caught. The wide eyes turned up to her were brown with patches of dark forest green.

His ward indeed. Cottingwith had some explaining to do.

"And who is your companion?" Edme asked the girl.

"This is Gertrude. My best friend in all the world." Tongue hanging, the dog plopped on its haunches at the mention of its name.

"Sally and Gertrude live in a cottage just through those trees," Cottingwith said, pointing. "Sally, may I expect to see Mrs. Ewell appearing on that path very soon?"

Mrs. Ewell. Was she his mistress? Former mistress—perhaps Sally's mother?

The girl bit her lip. "She's sleeping, uncle. But the note. The note—in your pocket. It said I must go out very early, before Filkins starts work. Father Christmas has left me an early present in the gardener's shed."

"And you were going on your own?"

She lifted a thin shoulder. "I didn't wish to bother Mrs. Ewell. She was coughing last night."

"I thought her cold was better."

"The medicine was helping but... I don't know."

Cottingwith continued to frown at the girl until she hung her head.

"Well, I'm glad that you brought the note to me. Come along and I'll have one of the gardeners open the shed for me. You know it's always kept locked. I don't know how Father Christmas would have entered there."

"He can go anywhere. Mrs. Ewell says he can even go down chimneys. He's magic, you know, sir."

"Miss Beecham, will you come with us?"

"To see magic? I wouldn't miss it."

* * *

TRENT'S STOMACH CHURNED AS HE LED THEM TO A service area at the side of the gardens where a large shed housed shovels, spades, rakes, and the fertilizers and other supplies used to maintain the estate gardens. The shed was new, sturdy, well-maintained, and locked at the end of every day.

As they came round a hedge, he spotted Filkins, the head gardener, standing in front of the door. Trent caught Sally's arm before she could run ahead and led her and Edme to a nearby wooden bench.

"If you ladies would but have a seat here," he said, dusting the wooden slats with his handkerchief, "I'll see what's what and return."

Sally opened her mouth to object, and he gave her his sternest look—not always easy to do with the precious girl.

"Miss Sally," Miss Beecham said, pulling a bundle

55

from her pocket, "I have something here that will help us while away the time, if ye'd like some."

He sent her a grateful look and called a greeting to Filkins.

"My lord." Filkins turned and fumbled his hat. "Can't think what happened here. T'padlock's broken."

"Have you gone in?"

"Just arrived, my lord."

Trent brushed past him. "Allow me." He pushed the door open.

Dim light flickered in through the open door and small windows. As his vision adjusted to the poor lighting, shock flared into rage.

A fat mouse sporting a red bow lay dead, perched on a crate just inside the doorway. Sally was terrified of mice. It was why he'd given her Gertrude.

This wasn't vermin that got into the arsenic. That was locked up elsewhere.

Behind him, he heard Filkins's growl. "What the..."

"Who might have put this here, Filkins?"

"Damned if I know, my lord. And why?"

He turned on the man. Filkins had served Furningwood since his youth. He'd been shunned by the others because he'd joined the Methodists and turned away from the locals' smuggling. Trent had raised his wages and made him head gardener. He was one of the few servants he trusted.

56

Filkins had also become a friend to the little girl waiting outside, who, during the summer past, had followed him about asking questions and chattering.

"Sally received a note that Father Christmas left her an early gift here."

Filkins's face darkened. "What villain would do such a thing? The poor lass. We'll find out who, my lord."

"Quietly, though. For her sake, make no fuss. And let me deal with the culprit if you find him."

Or her.

Trent searched in his pocket and pulled out a coin. "We'll say we found this, alright?"

"A fivepence. That's a treasure for a wee one. I'll get this mess cleaned."

Trent found his ladies with a small piece of oilcloth spread out on Miss Beecham's lap.

Sally leapt up. "Uncle," she cried, "was it there? Was my present there?"

He held up the coin and her face fell.

"Sally," he said, "are you disappointed?"

She bit her lips and shook her head. "It's only that I was hoping for a doll."

"But that's a fivepence," Miss Beecham cried. "Why, Sally, ye might buy yourself sweets with that."

Her face brightened. "Mr. Crawford's shop has sweets. Oh, but Mrs. Ewell won't take me, not if she's coughing. Would you, uncle?"

He hadn't thought ahead to the demands a coin

57

burning a hole in a little girl's reticule might generate. Yet, why not? He'd thought to have Sally attend the children's party, but a shopping trip into the village would be a perfect way to introduce her to the house party guests.

"There are still a few days until Christmas," he said. "We'll plan a trip into the village, shall we?"

Sally jumped up and down, in danger of dropping the coin. "I wonder if it will be enough for the doll in Mr. Crawford's window. Oh, what if I can't find anything for a fivepence?"

He'd also forgotten how greedy children could be.

Edme winked up at him. "Perhaps ye might buy a small gift for someone else. Your nursemaid, or his lordship."

Sally sent him a puzzled frown. "But we have something for you now, uncle. Look, we saved you a piece of shortbread."

A lone square of biscuit nestled in Miss Beecham's lap. He didn't dare reach for it.

His lady took pity upon him and with a smile, lifted the cloth up to him.

He took a bite. The rich buttery flavor with its hint of sweetness was as delectable as the lady in front of him.

"Delicious. My compliments to your cook." He shoved the rest of it into his mouth.

"My lady made it herself," Sally said, "and she's going to teach me how to make some."

"With his lordship's and Mrs. Ewell's permission," Miss Beecham said.

He dusted his hands. "You have it, providing you make a batch for me."

Color rose under the freckles on Edme's cheeks as she glanced away; a deeper color than that roused by the cold morning air.

And it was cold. In fact, the morning clouds had not lifted, and the air tasted of rain.

"Sally, I'm not 'my lady'. I'm Miss Beecham. Can ye remember that?"

"Miss Beecham. Miss Beecham. Like trees or the sand by the water."

Trent tugged the little girl's cloak closed. "Come, Sally, I'm taking you home."

"You must come too, Miss Beecham."

Trent frowned. "If Mrs. Ewell is ill—"

"Then I can look after Sally while ye send for help," she said.

His heart lifted. Miss Edme Beecham, with her gleaming bronze hair and her sparkling amber eyes was a treasure, inside and out.

"SALLY BROWN." THE INDIGNANT CRY CAME FROM A stout older woman bundled up to her eyeballs.

59

Huffing up the walk, she punctuated her arrival with a deep cough.

Edme let out a long breath, and a feeling of giddiness came over her. Mrs. Ewell was definitely not a current or former mistress.

Sally hung her head and clung to the tail of Cottingwith's coat.

"I'm sorry milord," the woman said in a thick London accent. "Stuffed a pillow under her blanket, she did, and out the window she went while I was frying up eggs. Sally Brown, I ought ter—"

Another wracking cough cut off Mrs. Ewell's proposed punishment.

Edme exchanged a look with Cottingwith. "That cough sounds deep, Ma'am. Mayhap ye'll allow me to escort you back to the cottage, while his lordship has a word with wee naughty Sally."

She linked arms with the astonished woman, and they set out together. "I have younger brothers, Ma'am. I ken your wish to give her a birching."

"Aye, but I won't. The earl won't allow it."

"Nor would my da where I was concerned. But the boys?" She shook her head. "Sally had cause for what she did." She told her about the note and the fivepence. "She must be a smart little whippet, reading already."

"Aye, she is that. And a good enough girl except that she—well, she's lonely. She needs other young 'uns around. Someone to play with."

Sally was lonely. "The earl's promised to take her shopping, though I'll advise him to hold off until tomorrow, as a punishment. Providing you're well enough to look after her."

"Oh, I'm better, miss. The cold air makes the cough worse, is all."

Edme saw the cottage through the trees, a snug, homely dwelling. Inside, Mrs. Ewell directed her to the sitting room flanking one side of the small hall, but she followed the warmth and smell of cooking to the kitchen in back.

"See here," Mrs. Ewell beckoned her to a door. Tucked up next to the kitchen and warmed by the cookfire was a small bedchamber where Sally slept.

Edme couldn't help laughing. "Clever lass." The bundle under the covers did indeed look like a sleeping child.

A CHASTENED SALLY APOLOGIZED TO HER CARETAKER and while Edme sipped a cup of tea, the girl sat down to her toast, eggs, and oatmeal, feeding bits of bread to Gertrude when she thought Edme wasn't looking.

She hid her smile and looked around. The kitchen was well appointed, the furnishings plain but well-made. And the Christmas spirit was everywhere in pine boughs, ribbon, and chains of colored paper.

Cottingwith had taken Mrs. Ewell to the parlor and closed the door.

"Tell me about the doll you were wishing for," Edme said.

The girls eyes lit. "Oh, she's beautiful. I saw her at the mercantile. She has yellow hair and blue eyes and she's so beautiful."

"Ye don't want a doll with brown hair like yours?"

"Oh, I have one. Uncle gave me one last summer for my birthday. But Herbert said it was ugly, like me."

Dastard. "How long has Herbert been blind?" Edme asked.

"H-he's not."

"He must be to say such a thing. Or... does he fancy ye? Sometimes boys say mean things because they fancy a lass and want her attention. Why, my brothers—"

"Herbert's not a boy." She shook her head fiercely.

"He's a man?"

Sally nodded.

What sort of man insulted a child? He ought to be horsewhipped. Or gelded, yes that would do.

"From the village?"

She shook her head.

"From the home farm?"

"No."

Edme leaned across the table. "Out with it, lass."

"From the manor. He's a footman."

How in heaven's name had the child run into a footman from the manor?

Before she could ask, Cottingwith and the housekeeper joined them. She looked as chastened as Sally had earlier, whereas his lordship wore his familiar staid expression.

They would go shopping on the morrow, Cottingwith promised, if Mrs. Ewell reported Sally had been on good behavior the rest of the day.

A few minutes later, Edme and Cottingwith stepped out of the cottage into air that had grown even colder.

"What did ye find in that shed?" she asked, holding onto his arm, as if she'd have any choice about it the way he was gripping her.

A cloud came over him. "A dead mouse tied with a red ribbon. Living or dead, they terrify Sally."

"*What?*" Anger gripped her. Who would play such a cruel prank on a child? Perhaps it was that Herbert from the Manor. There was a story here, no doubt, one she'd get out of Cottingwith before the week was out.

"Can we not bring Sally up to the manor house?"

He crossed his arms and frowned, a hard look coming over him. She'd seen him serious before, but never fearsome. Not that he frightened her—she had too many brothers to be blown over by a man's angry face. Besides, in her gut she knew the anger wasn't directed at her.

Part of that story he must tell her.

"Not yet."

"No, I suppose not. She was naughty after all, and she has to pay some price for that."

He fixed her with a searching, almost haunted, look. "I will tell you everything, I promise. Naughty though she is, she's but an innocent child."

His innocent child. And he cared for her, Edme could see that. She'd never have expected such... such vulnerability in such a reserved man.

Such a good man, perhaps, despite the fact that he'd disappointed her last year.

They saw the head gardener coming their way.

She touched Cottingwith's hand. "I'll hold ye to your promise, my lord."

"My name is Trenton," he said. "My most intimate friends call me Trent."

Intimate. The mere word sent a gush of warmth through her body down to her nether regions.

Ah, well, she was a fool, wasn't she? Scottish, and a hoyden, raised with brothers. "And mine call me Edme. Ye may do so as well in private but have no illusions that we're on intimate terms."

He sent her a long look that had heat rolling through her again and said, "Not yet."

64

* * *

FILKINS HAD NOTHING TO REPORT ON THE MOUSE, BUT he'd heard Mrs. Ewell's coughing and sent a trusted man to fetch his elderly parents to pay a call on the cottage and allow the lady some rest.

Finding out who had played the prank was another matter. Despite the presence of guests, Trent would have to corner Mother and find out just what she knew of the matter.

She could be devious, his mother, but when confronted, she was a terrible liar who fell back on her dignity and her temper.

As they reached the gardening shed, a man hailed him.

Hatherot, with his sister on his arm, was advancing on them.

The marquess wished them a good morning. "You see, sister." He sent Lady Ottilia a sidewise glance. "I told you I'd have to get up early to steal a march on Cottingwith. And where did the two of you get off to before dawn this morning?" His eyes gleamed with faux humor. "Or did you depart the manor earlier than dawn?"

He heard Edme's gasp at the implication. Damn the fellow, he'd win Edme honorably, not by ruining her.

"Mr. Filkins," Edme said, her placid demeanor helping calm Trent's anger. "I thank ye for your tour this morn'. I expect we should let ye be about the business of tending to these lovely grounds."

What a gem she was. "Yes, thank you, Filkins," Trent said. "Hatherot, Lady Ottilia, the amaryllis are blooming in the greenhouse, is that not so, Filkins? You'll find that on the west side of the manor. And now, I've promised Miss Beecham her breakfast."

"You see that, sister? He means to dismiss us. But we shall accompany you to the breakfast room, Cottingwith."

They were the first to arrive, and Hatherot hurried to fetch a plate for Edme and seat her by him. Trent summoned his good manners and prepared a plate for Lady Ottilia, who had seated herself to the right of what she must have expected would be his seat at the head of the table.

His mother entered with Kinmarty in tow. Trent hastened to fill a plate for his mother, who took a seat at her usual place at the foot of the table.

Kinmarty joined him at the buffet. "Filomena will be down shortly after his nibs finishes his breakfast." He piled his plate with eggs, bacon, and kippers.

"You will take the seat at the head of the table," Trent murmured.

With a hasty glance, Kinmarty chuckled. "I shall pull rank on my host, shall I? Wicked good entertainment this week. Have you any more surprise guests arriving?"

Trent thought of Sally. He'd find a way to include her, despite her questionable origins.

That thought reminded him: two boys resided in Kinmarty's nursery, his brother's illegitimate sons. Trent hadn't thought to include them in his Yuletide invitation.

"Where are your nephews?" he asked.

"Have no fear. They're in town this week with Penelope."

"You ought to have brought them."

Kinmarty sent him a long look. "You're a decent fellow, Cottingwith."

He thought of the little girl he'd stashed away in a cottage. "Not as decent as you might think. I hope we might talk privately."

More guests entered, including the duchess.

"Certainly." The duke hurried to prepare his lady a plate.

CHAPTER FIVE

After a breakfast spent dodging Hatherot's sly questions and innuendos, Edme succumbed to their hostess's plans for the day—gathering more evergreens to decorate the manor. As if they didn't already have enough. But the Darnley lasses and lads had wink-winked about mistletoe, and Archie had joined in until Mrs. Yardley put a stop to their hijinks with a stern call to order.

The duke, Lord Darnley, and Lord Hatherot had quickly excused themselves to go riding.

At least she wouldn't have Hatherot annoying her this morning.

Nor Mrs. Yardley, who had no plans to brave the cold, gloomy day to fetch greens. She, the duchess, and Lady Darnley elected to stay behind. When the gatherers returned, though, they would help with the trimming.

Furningwood would host a dinner the next night and Mrs. Yardley had invited some of the local families. Over the next two days there'd be shopping in the nearby village for last minute gifts, a tour of the gardens and greenhouse, games, musicales, more dinners. On Christmas Eve, Furningwood would hold an afternoon party for the children of gentry, and a ball in the evening for neighbors and guests. Those guests who wished to and were able might attend morning service on Christmas day and return for dinner and a quiet afternoon preparing to depart the next morning before the Boxing Day party planned for tenants and servants.

Mrs. Yardley organized the younger guests into groups accompanied by footmen and grooms with their carts to carry back the haul. Edme went foraging with Archie, Simon Darnley and his sister Helen Darnley, while the older Darnley girl, Diana, and Lady Ottilia accompanied Hector Darnley and Cottingwith.

When she went to fetch her heavy mantle, Archie followed her to her room and slipped inside. Joanie arrived with an armful of freshly pressed gowns and made as if to leave, but Edme waved her in.

"Good morning, Joanie." Archie lounged against the bedpost. "Where did ye get off to this morning, oh sister dear?"

She shrugged. "I went for a walk."

"With our host?"

Archie's face was surprisingly serious.

"Yes."

"Without Joanie?"

"I offered to go, Mr. Archie," Joanie said. "But she insisted I stay here."

"As she would. Be careful, Edme. Even I have noticed Mrs. Yardley's withering looks toward ye. It's very clear she wants to keep your distracting self out of the way so Cottingwith may choose between Lady Ottilia..." he wrinkled his nose, "and one of the jolly Darnley girls."

"It's true." Joanie looked up from the chest where she was working, frowned and then pressed her lips together.

Edme shared a look with Archie. "Joanie, ye said the staff eats well, but are the servants as rude as the mistress?"

Joanie straightened to her full height and threw back her wide shoulders. "Not all. Two of the housemaids are almost friendly. The rest are standoffish if not downright cold. I ken there's bad blood between the earl and his mother, and mayhap the butler and housekeeper as well, though who's siding with who, I don't know. And I'm sorry, Miss Edme but it's true they don't want us Scots here. Never seen the likes of it. It wairn't like this at the duke's in London. It's glad I'll be when this week is over."

Bad blood. If Mrs. Yardley had put out that mouse for Sally, she was truly a vile human being.

Which reminded her... "Joanie, is there a footman named Herbert?"

The maid scrunched her nose. "Aye. Related to the butler he is. Nephew or summat."

"What does he look like?"

"What do any of 'em look like? Tall, well enough looking, dark hair under the half wig."

"Ye must point him out to me if ye're able."

Archie drew closer. "Why?"

"Thank ye for telling us, Joanie," she said. "Ye may tell anyone who asks that I'm here to discuss the shipping business."

Oh, but a courtship was underway, like it or not. What sort of life would she have with such a wicked woman as mother-in-law? It was yet another reason to put an end to the notion of courting.

"The same goes for me," Archie said. "On that note, Cottingwith wants to meet when we return from this mistletoe hunt. Let me help ye with that mantle."

LATER THAT AFTERNOON, ARCHIE AND EDME MADE their way to Cottingwith's study.

"What say ye, sister? Can we trust Cottingwith in the matter of this shipbuilding enterprise?"

They were meant to talk about ships, but she'd much rather send Archie away and learn more about the little girl in the cottage who had the same eyes as the earl.

"Or in any other matter?" he added, reading her mind. He raised an eyebrow. "After all, ye spent the last Yuletide with him at Kinmarty. What did ye learn of the man?"

"Not much." She shook her head. "Ann and I thought he was cold. Polite though, in a reserved sort of way."

"Cold?"

"Yes."

"Cold. Not cunning?"

They'd reached the door to the study, and Archie's gaze pinned her, raising her ire. But there was no time for a row with her brother, and she could do no less than be honest.

"Cold," she said. "Not cunning. Else he would have asked to court me before he ran away from Kinmarty instead of now."

Her brother's raised eyebrows and gaping mouth gave her a moment's satisfaction, and she rapped on the door and then turned the knob.

Cottingwith came around his desk and thanked them for skipping a nap and meeting with him.

Archie shook Cottingwith's hand affably. "We're

neither of us old enough to need naps, though I felt like a wee lad this morning. I haven't climbed so many trees in years. Simon and I fetched enough mistletoe to keep all the ladies happy. We quite outdid your team, Cottingwith, didn't we, Edme, and had fun despite our labors."

"Yes, indeed."

Cottingwith laughed. "So much so that we lost Hector and Miss Darnley to your group."

Lady Ottilia had torn her skirt and demanded the earl escort her back to the manor. The thought had raised a moment's jealousy in Edme, but she soon brought her emotions under control and set about enjoying herself. Cottingwith had deserted her once before, and if it were Lady Ottilia he wanted, well so be it.

She liked the young Darnleys. Neither Helen nor Diana seemed intent on marrying Cottingwith, or anyone else, not even Archie.

She wrinkled her nose. "And I was happy to have Hector and Diana join us to help keep the two nodcocks in line."

"Until the kissing began."

Cottingwith blinked and sent her a strange look.

Her heart did a flip and she wanted to giggle. He was jealous.

"'Twas because of the mistletoe and all in good fun," Archie said. "Wasn't it, Edme?"

"Mere pecks on the cheeks. They were merely

making us feel welcome. Now, as ye know, Archie and I are in trade." She smiled, imagining how his mother might react. "Let us put on our Beecham Trading hats and hear what more ye have to say about the ship works."

They took seats in front of his massive desk. He peered across at her, frowning. "I may have a title, Edme, but I'm in trade as well."

Archie lifted his eyebrows and sent her a questioning look.

"I've allowed his lordship the use of my first name," she said. "Ye don't mind, do ye, Archie?"

"Hmm." Archie rubbed his chin. "First names. My lord, shall we talk about your ship works, or something else? Something more personal, more in the way of a merger?"

She could feel the color rising in her cheeks. She would box Archie's ears if he kept bringing up personal matters. "We're talking about the Yardley-Jelson ship works, isn't that right, my lord?"

"Archie, talks of another sort of merger are, I fear, premature." Cottingwith directed a warm look her way. "I promised to show you plans today." He opened a drawer and pulled out a rolled sheaf of papers. "In my naval days—"

"Naval days?" Edme asked. "You didn't mention naval service before."

"I went to sea at the age of fourteen. When the war ended, I was let go along with many others. I worked for a chandler before I inherited, and then I had a time putting Furningwood in order. The estate trades in wool, beef, mutton, and bricks from our own brickworks. It was the bricks that introduced me to the Jelson works. Thomas Jelson is one of my old shipmates, son and grandson of shipwrights down Dover way."

"He knows the trade as well?" Edme asked.

"Yes. Grew up in the works, and he's brought his father along to Frindsbury. He didn't go off to sea until the last few years of the war. They've moved the works closer to Chatham because... It seems Dover fell out of favor with the King when his lady wife returned for the coronation, and the town welcomed her back with open arms."

Edme exchanged a glance with Archie. Their father had schooled them well on the subject of the royals. Though King George and his brothers and sisters and late wife were often fodder for jokes, a man—or woman—in business had best not mention those jokes in public.

"Jelson has been sustaining the business by building Thames yachts and barges for cargoes like our bricks. For a while, they had a good number of orders for hoys for the, er, free traders. The coastal patrols have put a dent in that market."

"Is smuggling another one of the Furningwood businesses?" Archie asked.

Edme watched with interest as Cottingwith's

finger moved soundlessly, tapping the desktop. He lifted his gaze to her.

"Yes, in all honesty, when I inherited, it was. There were great profits for my uncle and cousin, one of the reasons they could be so profligate. The local people benefited as well during the war years."

The Beechams were no lovers of the Excise Officers and their taxes, but the goods offered by free traders cut into their own legitimate trade. That was another topic they didn't discuss publicly. "And now?" Edme asked.

"And now, the brandy doesn't flow as freely at Furningwood."

He was dodging. She opened her mouth to tell him that, but Archie spoke first.

"And so, you're looking to what? Sell ships to Beecham Trading?" Archie asked.

"The market is flooded with decommissioned naval ships being sold for a song," Edme said.

"Very true, Edme. But those are sailing ships. We mean to continue building barges and small yachts while we transition to steam. Jelson worked for a time up in Rotherhithe on the Arrow, a wooden paddle steamer. He has ideas for a new design."

A knock came at the door, and the stern middle-aged man who served as butler simply opened the door and walked in.

Cottingwith frowned. "Yes, Taylor?"

"Mrs. Yardley requests your presence in the drawing room."

"Tell her I'll be along presently."

The older man cleared his throat. "Two of your guests, Lord Hatherot and his sister are there as well and wish your company."

"And they shall have my company presently. Close the door when you leave."

What a rude staff Cottingwith had.

Taylor's lips pressed into a tight line and with one final disdainful look, he left.

Joanie's observations of a civil war between master and mistress were proved true, and Cottingwith apparently exercised little authority over his butler. How competent was he at managing his businesses?

She watched the movement of his long fingers as he unrolled the sheaf of papers. Archie pulled up his chair, eager to see and raptly attentive to Cottingwith's explanations. The industry would move to steam for commercial transport, but the problem with wooden ships was the danger of fire. Jelson had developed designs for boiler improvements and a steel hull.

They'd heard some of this from him the night before. Now, while her own eyes glazed over, Archie asked questions with the sagacity of an engineer. This was a side of her usually frivolous brother that she'd never seen. Cottingwith answered with patience and his own reserved sort of enthusiasm.

"You're quiet, Edme," Cottingwith said, finally. "Do you have questions?"

"I don't know enough to speculate whether that steel hull will sink. What I'd like, er, what William will want to know is the costs involved for the steel and the laborers, as well as who will want to buy such a ship, and what interest you've had in ordering."

"All fair questions." He pulled up another folder, but just then the door opened again.

"There you are." Mrs. Yardley took a step in, turning a glare on Edme that sent her own temper sparking.

Cottingwith rose and Archie leapt to his feet, but Edme remained seated.

Hatherot crowded in behind Mrs. Yardley. "I've been waiting for you old chum." The marquess's gaze strayed to the plans. Cottingwith set his hand on the paper.

"Mother," Cottingwith said, "Please show Hatherot to the library. The latest newspapers will have arrived by now, Hatherot, and you may help yourself to cigars and brandy. I'll be along to join you."

Mrs. Yardley bristled. "Why, Cottingwith, all of your guests are in the drawing room waiting for you."

His jaw hardened and he raised an eyebrow; Edme wondered if that was the closest he came to an outburst of anger.

"I'll join them presently, Mother. But two of my guests are here, as you can see, and we haven't finished our conversation." He lazily rolled up the designs for the new ship.

Hatherot chuckled, avidly watching the scene playing out, the cur.

'Twas no wonder Cottingwith locked all the doors to his study. She doubted the marquess had any sort of mind for business or money to invest. He could, however, easily convey a new design about to be patented to a competitor—for the right price.

"Oh, do come along," Mother said. "Miss Beecham, we need an extra hand tying ribbons."

Edme studied the strong hand and long fingers rolling the papers and a tingle went through her. Cottingwith was a braw man, but one fighting a battle that wasn't physical, something more than the ties of his mother's apron strings. Perhaps all the players weren't known, but some were: the butler and many of the staff had turned against him and allied themselves with his mother.

Why? Had he cut their wages? Money often played a hand in such conflicts. Or... was it something to do with the smuggling?

If the last two earls had been engaged in free trading, perhaps Mrs. Yardley thought access to fine goods at low costs would raise her place in society. Filomena said the Yardleys were not high *ton*. Cottingwith's father had been an earl's younger son, true, but he'd married a woman from a gentry family.

The lass in the brick cottage and this harpy of a mother were grounds enough for Edme to refuse a courtship. Not to mention, such distractions would not make Cottingwith a sound business partner, and that message she'd convey to William as soon as she could put pen to paper.

"Miss Beecham," his mother said with no little indignation.

"Mother, we will be along presently." Cottingwith had gentled his tone, but Edme heard the steel behind it.

His patience was fraying. All alone in this manor house with businesses to run and a little girl to protect from tormentors who might include his own mother?

He wasn't all alone now.

A girl wishing to be courted would woo the mother as well, wouldn't she? But never mind courtship; justice demanded this lady be put in her place. She must do so carefully though.

"Ma'am." Edme drew herself up in her seat and forced a smile. "My brother and I have made note of your exceptionable, *er, exceptional* courtesy."

She heard a gurgling noise from the vicinity of

Mrs. Yardley, but she cast a gaze at Cottingwith. He was watching her intently.

She smiled—this time genuinely—and turned back to Mrs. Yardley. "Our brother, in fact, accepted the earl's kind invitation to visit Furningwood with the express understanding that we'd speak in person about mutual business interests, as well as enjoy the rare pleasure of celebrating an English Christmas. We beg a bit more of your courtesy. I promise ye I'll hurry along and tie ribbons until midnight if need be, as soon as this meeting with Cottingwith has concluded."

Archie's lips twitched. "We shan't be long," he said with an affected aristocratic drawl. "I'm anxious to hang the mistletoe Simon and I went to such great pains to harvest."

Hatherot smirked and raised an eyebrow. "Buried in all that treacle, Miss Beecham, is the notion that your brother sent the two of you to represent him? Can that be true?"

"Yes," Mrs. Yardley bristled. "We're to believe—"

"As she said," Cottingwith said. "Now, if you please... Mother, Hatherot." He made a shooing notion.

Thoroughly rude, but didn't those two deserve it?

Hatherot chuckled. "Perhaps it's something I'd be interested—"

"Perhaps," Edme said, though there was no way the Beechams would have any financial ties with

Hatherot. "Ye may ask Cottingwith about it later. For now, we'll speak with him privately. Thank ye, my lord, ma'am for your courtesy and understanding. We will be along presently."

Cottingwith was halfway across the room when she'd finished her speech, escorting his mother to the door.

* * *

TRENT TURNED THE KEY IN THE LOCK AND RETURNED to the desk.

Edme Beecham had depths he hadn't seen last Christmas at Castle Kinmarty. Oh, he'd seen her kindness and intelligence, but he hadn't known she'd have so much backbone.

She would make a fine countess. The servants would fall into line, or she'd let them go.

Edme reached for the file. "May I?"

"Please. And I apologize for—"

"Your mother's rudeness?"

"Yes." His mother was damnably rude and more.

Archie laughed. "I've never seen my sister issue a set down so politely before. Edme is usually far more direct, Cottingwith. I suppose she was cushioning the blow because it was your mother."

"I'm sitting right here," Edme said. "Mrs. Yardley is our hostess, Archie, nothing more to me than that."

"Yes. And no fool, I imagine. She'll have seen what ye were about. I suppose we'll pay the price. What say ye, Cottingwith? Will there be arsenic in the pudding?"

Edme closed the file and looked up. "And a dead mouse in the Christmas stocking, Cottingwith? I believe we are finished here."

She'd barely had time to scan a few pages. That had been no thorough review.

Archie stood, looking older and more serious than his eighteen years. "Cottingwith, would ye prefer we remove ourselves to a local inn? We can continue our negotiations there."

"Hades." He jumped to his feet and crossed to the French door. Clouds had settled over the landscape deepening the early twilight. "No. Please don't leave. And, Edme, please don't set yourself against my proposal just yet."

Either one of his proposals.

"William was keen enough on this deal to send us all the way to Kent," Archie said, "so yes, of course, we'll hear ye out. Isn't that so, Edme?"

She pressed her eyes closed for a moment, took a deep breath, and said "Yes."

Edme's temper had flared—Trent had seen her color rising—yet she hadn't fallen into a snit. Thank heavens for Archie's reminder and her own good sense. "Thank you. I'd like to escort you to Chatham after Christmas and meet with Jelson at the works."

"So be it." Edme nodded. "It's what William would do. In the meantime, I will need time with the books."

"Of course."

"And may I see the books on your brick works as well? 'Twill help me reassure William of your business acumen."

She'd poked out her chin as if she thought he'd object, the cheeky lass. In fact, he didn't mind at all. Perhaps if she saw him as a good businessman and provider, she'd forgive him and be more receptive to his wooing.

"If they're at the works, mayhap your manager or steward or secretary could find them for me."

"I have them here. My steward deals only with the agricultural operations, and I'm without a secretary for the moment."

Was this the time to bring up that subject? Things were moving along more quickly than he expected.

"In fact, I'll be hiring a new secretary very soon."

Archie sat up in his chair, but it was Edme's curious look that grabbed his attention.

Imagine having her seated at the small desk across the room, day in and day out, handling his affairs.

He'd never get a bit of work done. No, his aspirations for her were far different, and far more important.

"Would you be interested?" he asked, directing

the question to Archie. "It would be something different than trading. While my land steward oversees his part, you'd necessarily have an overview of those operations, as well as the businesses and my parliamentary work. I imagine I'll need to be more engaged there."

Archie glanced at his sister.

She frowned. "What happened to the previous incumbent, my lord?"

"He found other employment." It had been a hell of a year since his visit to Castle Kinmarty.

"Why does that sound portentous?" Archie asked.

"There were funds missing. And the Riding Officer visited the vacant dower house." Fortunately, they'd not found anything there, but only because Trent had personally helped to empty the items stashed by the gang. Several local men had been arrested though, and the blame for it placed on Trent. He hadn't reported them, but neither had he been willing to use his title or his coin to influence the Riding Officer, as the previous earls had done.

"Archie, I suspect the earl is trying to wean the locals from the free trading," Edme said.

"Yes." He nodded.

"With the increased coastal patrols, it's become far too dangerous," she said.

Clever girl, but that wasn't the only reason. "I'd prefer to see the people I'm responsible for support their families without risking transportation or worse."

She looked away and took a deep breath. "And what of that other matter, my lord?"

His conversation with Mother that morning had been interrupted by Taylor, but she'd denied any involvement. He'd seen the lie in her eyes, though. If she hadn't instigated the prank herself, she knew who had.

Edme's gaze searched him. Dammit, he owed her an explanation for Sally, for his abrupt departure last winter, for his mother's rudeness. How else could he ever gain her trust?

"Archie, might I have a word alone with your sister?"

"Unchaperoned? William would have my—"

"Step onto the terrace," Edme said. "Ye can watch through the window. Cottingwith is not the sort to molest a girl, especially not one looking into his books."

Her teasing manner eased his nerves. He pulled a cheroot from the box in his drawer and handed it to Archie whose eyes lit.

"Very well," Archie said. "I'll be watching."

Trent fetched a spill and helped him light the tobacco, then ushered him out the French door and returned to take the seat Archie had vacated. He turned the chair to face Edme and took both of her hands in his.

Archie had walked to the balustrade and had his back to them.

"My mother denies any knowledge of the note to Sally or the dead mouse. I don't believe her, but I need a private moment and more time to press her. Filkins has sent word that he hasn't learned anything yet, which tells me it's likely a house servant behind this.

She furrowed her brows. "'Tis against ye, Cottingwith, this cowardly action. No sane person would do such a thing to an innocent child. Ye care for her, and they strike out at ye through her."

His mother wanted Sally gone. Had she exceeded the bounds of sanity in her obsession with rank and social standing?

The squeeze on his hand drew his attention to her. "What is Sally to ye, my lord?"

His fingers itched to trace the curve of her cheek. The gaze she turned on him held no accusation, only curiosity, and dare he hope, concern. For himself or for Sally, it didn't matter.

"I promised you an explanation for why I left Kinmarty so suddenly last Christmas."

"And so," she whispered, "what happened?"

He sighed and studied her hands, so small and feminine, and then raised his gaze to meet hers. "Sally," he said. "Sally happened. She needed me quite desperately."

CHAPTER SIX

*E*dme held very still as the grip of his hands tightened on hers, as tight as the self-control he was exercising, despite the powerful emotions swamping him.

She waited to learn if he would tell her the truth, for if he couldn't, she could never respect, much less trust him.

"Sally calls me uncle, but in fact, I believe... No, she *is* my daughter."

Relief flooded her, relief and compassion and... no, this warm feeling wasn't, couldn't be, love. One conversation wasn't enough to wipe away last year's hurt. What if he left without explanation again, as he might?

Oh heavens. She freed a hand and touched his cheek, sweeping a thumb over his afternoon bristles. When he raised her other hand and pressed his lips to her palm, a delicious burn traveled up her arm, making her shiver.

"I mean to marry you, Edme." The green pools amidst the brown of his eyes darkened. "If you'll have me after you hear the rest."

Grateful for the reminder not to lose herself this day, she folded her hands in her lap and listened to a sorry tale, one that might have happened to any young man with a caring heart.

Cottingwith had been working as a ship's chandler when a childhood friend's widow reached out for help. She'd followed the drum to Portugal and later Spain, France, and Flanders, and then returned to England with her husband, who was living a half-life due to wounds he'd received at Waterloo. In the months before he died, they'd run through most of their funds. Both her family and his rejected her; she was making do as a seamstress, living in dun territory near Greenwich when she encountered Trent—who was not yet Cottingwith—working there.

He'd helped her find better lodgings and provided her money, and though it had never been his intention, he'd fallen into a brief affair with her, one that he immediately regretted.

Called to work in Portsmouth for a time, he'd continued to send her funds. By then she'd written that she was with child.

His or her late husband's, she wasn't sure.

"You... you didn't offer to marry her?" Edme held her breath, her emotions in conflict. A gentleman would have proposed, though if he'd married the woman... She forced down a flare of jealousy.

"I did offer. She refused. You might think it shameful, but I was grateful. When Sally was born, I went down to see her, to satisfy my conscience, I suppose. Sally had wispy blond hair and dark blue eyes, like her mother's late husband, so I didn't think she was mine."

"A newborn's eyes—"

"Yes," he said. "Sometimes change colors." Cottingwith sighed. "Before her confinement, her mother had moved into a country cottage with another officer's widow, an older woman who was childless and thrilled to have a baby to look after."

He grimaced, and she waited.

"Relieved of most of the childcare, Sally's mother began to drink. Sally was three when her mother died. For the sake of my late friend, I'd continued to send money, and I went on paying the widow to keep Sally. On my rare visits, Sally seemed happy, well cared for, and loved."

"But..."

"My cousin died, and I inherited. I was busy with Furningwood, with the brick works, the plans for the ship works, and trying to draw the locals away from the free trade. I hadn't visited since the summer before last."

He bit his lip. "I ought to have visited. Just before Christmas last, Sally's caretaker fell ill and died rather suddenly. When Sally finally reached neighbors for help and returned... it was winter in the country. They'd always had problems with vermin and she was never afraid before but... it wasn't a pretty sight."

A shiver went through Edme. "Mice?"

He nodded. "She was hysterical, the neighbors said. The day I left Kinmarty, I'd received an express from my solicitor who handled the payments to Sally's caretaker, and all I could think of was reaching her. By that time... well you've seen her. She has the Yardley eyes. She's mine."

Edme frowned, thinking. "Who knew about the mice?"

"I've run through the list wondering. My solicitor of course, Mrs. Ewell, and anyone *she* told."

"Your gardener?" Edme asked. "He seemed to know."

"No. He'd have to be a very good actor to be the villain who put them there."

"Your mother?"

He squeezed his eyes closed. She could only imagine what sort of scene his mother had caused. "She'd spent last Christmas alone at Furningwood, getting the house in order, as she said, and getting to know the local gentry, deciding who would enhance her social aspirations. I traveled south as quickly as

91

possible. By the time I reached London, my solicitor had hired Mrs. Ewell to care for Sally and put them in temporary lodgings. The cottage where she's living had been used by the locals for storing contraband."

His long pause told her that clearing out the free traders had not been a popular move.

"I hoped Mother would come to know Sally and adjust to her presence. Mother objected, even after I told her Sally's unfortunate story."

"Did you tell her the whole truth?"

"Not in so many words."

Edme searched his eyes. "And she told her maid Sally's story, who told the butler who told the housekeeper, and everyone knows."

"My first mistake was to not start as I meant to go on."

"How did you mean to go on?"

"I meant to move Sally into the nursery and let the news trickle out that she's mine. Between Sally's tantrums and my mother's, I decided to wait."

Edme shook her head. "Children have tantrums. It's the way of things. But adults… Your mother is a snob, Cottingwith. For my part, I know that the duke and duchess won't be scandalized by your illegitimate child."

He reached for hers again. "And what of Edme Beecham? Have I lost her good opinion forever?"

The large strong hands swallowing her own smaller ones made her feel safe, secure, stable.

Was that a deception? He waited, unflinching, for her to speak.

Sally Brown was just a child. Edme had older brothers and didn't believe for a second that any one of them might never have fathered a bastard. Perhaps they had, and she didn't know about it, or they didn't know either, or they'd simply been lucky.

Men and women both made mistakes. But a man wasn't a man if he didn't care for his offspring. Would she be any better than his mother if she shunned Sally Brown?

She leaned closer. "Ye've been foolish, Cottingwith, and impulsive, and…" A coward where his mother was concerned.

But she couldn't say the word. He wasn't truly a coward. His mother was bossy, and he'd done the right thing despite her. Perhaps he truly loved the woman who'd given him birth.

"Your mother is rude, but is she really so wicked as to terrorize her own grandchild?"

"It's fear ruling her, I'm afraid. I never told her Sally is mine, but she suspects."

"Of course, she suspects, ye great lummox. She's your mother."

"Great lummox." He leaned in and his lips brushed against hers, and then, unlike last night's interrupted kiss, lingered.

Soft and dry, the sensation shocked her, igniting her senses. His lips tasted of a recent cheroot, the flavor mixing with the scent of starch and the faint manly odor of his morning shaving soap. She'd been kissed before, wet sloppy kisses that sent her reeling, and not in a good way. But this...

She gripped his arm and pressed closer, reveling in the feel, and the movement, and the warm desire curling through her. When he set his hand to the back of her head and pressed his tongue to the seam of her lips, she opened for him, marveling at how good the invasion felt.

Oh yes, she'd been kissed like that before as well, but had never enjoyed it, had quickly withdrawn.

She slid both hands to the back of his neck and plunged her fingers into his thick locks.

Tap-tap-tap.

Cottingwith groaned, pulled away a moment, and kissed his way down to the curve of her neck.

Tap-tap-tap.

He pulled her hands from his neck, sat back, and sent a rueful glance to the French door. And then alarm flashed in his face. With a quick squeeze of her hands, he jumped up.

Her back had been to the door, but what she saw sent her to her feet. Archie peered through the glass, and just under him were two more sets of eyes and one wet nose. Sally was here along with her dog Gertrude.

* * *

THE DEVIL. TRENT HURRIED TO THE DOOR. COULD HE not find one blessed person competent enough to mind a little girl and keep her safe?

When he opened the door, Gertrude bounced in demanding a pat. Edme intercepted the dog and ruffled her ears while he bent to greet Sally.

"I've found one of your tenants," Archie said. "Just in the nick of time, I'd say," he added muttering.

Trent would deal with Archie later. "Sally, my dear." He crouched in front of her. "Where is Mr. Filkins? You were supposed to stay with him."

"Gertrude had to go out to…" She waggled her hand. "You know. And Mrs. Filkins was in the parlor with Mrs. Ewell talking. And old Mr. Filkins was taking a nap in the chair. Mrs. Ewell always says not to bother the grownups when they're, er busy."

Anger thickened his throat. A child's safety was more important than good manners.

"Why didn't you stay near the cottage and take Gertrude in right away?"

Sally hung her head and lifted a shoulder.

"Ye went to the gardener's shed, didn't ye, Sally?" Edme had joined him in front of the child, her voice firm, but still kind.

She would be a wonderful mother to his children.

Sally lifted her chin, and the look she gave Edme

was searching, questioning, and almost defiant. "Are you going to marry my uncle?" Sally cringed back after asking the question, and Trent's heart broke.

Was Mrs. Ewell striking her? He'd specifically forbidden it.

Edme blinked. "Would ye mind very much if I did?"

Sally screwed up her lips, and he saw the uncertainty on her little face.

"I will tell ye this, Sally Brown. If the earl and I were to marry, ye'd not be living in the cottage, but here in the nursery, in the manor house, with the earl and me."

"And Gertrude?"

Edme fondled the dog's ears. "Of course."

"But there'll be no more running off alone with Gertrude," Trent said. "Now, let me take you and Gertrude home."

"I'll go along with ye," Archie said. "We have something to discuss, Cottingwith. On the way back perhaps is better."

"Lock up here first," Edme said. "I'll make excuses to your mother and your guests."

Just like his countess would do.

Archie took Sally's hand and led her outside.

She thought of Cottingwith's promise to take Sally shopping in the morning, if she behaved.

"What of the shopping tomorrow in the morn?" she asked.

"It's out of the question now." He hastily locked up the documents they'd been reviewing.

When he turned to go, she touched his arm and stayed him. "I would normally agree. She's a wee lass with spirit. One who's not being looked after properly there. She'll be easier to keep track of in the nursery here."

He shook his head. "Not until I've determined who I can trust to look after her here."

"Ye can trust *me* while ye smoke out your answer. And I happen to have a very large suite of rooms for some reason. I'll talk to Filomena. She brought a nursemaid for wee Lithgow. And my maid, Joanie, is not truly a lady's maid, but one of our housemaids who had plenty of experience wrangling my brothers."

He stowed his key in his pocket and touched her cheek. "You are a lovely, lovely woman, Edme Beecham."

Cold air rushed in through the open door. Archie and Sally held hands, swinging them back and forth until Sally laughed, but Archie glanced back and sent Trent a frown.

"Your brother is watching. I'd best go ask his permission to marry you."

Marriage. Her breath left in a whoosh, and a long moment passed whilst his thumb stirred up goosebumps.

"He's my little brother," she said, finally able to

speak, "and he has no say in the matter. Which still doesn't mean I've said yes."

* * *

EDME ATTACHED HERSELF TO FILOMENA IN THE drawing room but spotted Lady Ottilia carrying her spool of ribbon to come and join them.

"I must speak with you privately," Edme whispered. "Later."

Filomena nodded and greeted Lady Ottilia.

"Your brother outdid himself with the mistletoe," Lady Ottilia said pointing to the pile of greenery in front of Edme. Someone, a servant, Edme suspected, had formed them into kissing balls of different sizes, and it was her job to decorate them with ribbons.

"'Tis one Sassenach custom Archie fully embraces. Ouch." She rubbed the finger she'd just pricked. "I fear ye're much better at this than I am, Fil."

"How did you both become acquainted?" Lady Ottilia asked.

Edme told her about growing up with her cousin Ann, whose father had come back from India with great wealth. He'd whisked Ann away from the Beecham family and carried her off to the Highlands, where he expected her to make a match with the new Duke of Kinmarty.

"Unfortunately, I was in the way of that match,"

Filomena said. "I'd taken the job as housekeeper at Kinmarty, with a mind to make amends with my cousin, Penelope MacDonal who was traveling to Kinmarty, having also just returned from India. Penelope is the widow of Andrew's older brother."

"You were the housekeeper?" Lady Ottilia's eyes went impossibly wide.

"Not a very good one, but yes, for a short time." Filomena grinned. "Have I shocked you?"

"And it was love at first sight?"

"A bit more complicated than that. In truth, I despised Andrew. I'd hated him for so many years for something he'd done a long, long time ago, that it had become a bad habit."

"But, how did you…?"

"Patch things up? He apologized, and I forgave him."

Lady Ottilia stared for a long time at the piece of ribbon before her.

"It wasn't that simple of course. My dower was pitifully small—I'd been widowed the year before. Fortunately, Penelope *did* arrive from India, and she brought great wealth and a willingness to share it with me and her brother-in-law." Filomena sighed. "Christmas is a good time for forgiving those who've hurt us, isn't it?"

Edme caught her sly smile and pricked her finger again, gasping.

"You're right, your grace," Lady Ottilia said. "But how does one get the other party to apologize?"

"In our case, I found that I had something to apologize for as well. Ah." Fil set aside her scissors. "There is my maid signaling. His little lordship is demanding my appearance."

When she'd departed, Lady Ottilia turned to Edme, a question on her face.

"She's nursing the little marquess," Edme said, and then laughed. "Are you shocked again?"

"Yes." Lady Ottilia smiled, and then laughed. "Pleasantly so. Now, you must tell me all about Edinburgh, if you will, Miss Beecham. And do not worry, your brother is far too young for me. I have no designs on him or..." she leaned close and dropped her voice to a whisper, "our host."

Heat rushed to Edme's cheeks.

"Edinburgh," Lady Ottilia said. "Is it true what I read in Louis Simond's traveler's journal, that ladies go about barefoot there?"

"SALLY IS YOURS?"

Light flickered as Trent lifted his gaze from the dark path ahead, jostling the lantern he carried. He ought to have expected Archie Beecham's question after the lad's attentiveness to Sally.

"Yes. And before you ask, I've told Edme everything."

"Edme, hmm. You're courting my sister?"

"Yes, if she'll allow it."

"If she won't allow it than why were you kissing her?" He heard the lad's soft chuckle. "Though I suppose it's a good strategy. Edme thinks you're cold."

Cold? He was on fire for the lady. He wanted her in his bed, as his wife.

Trent held his tongue.

"As it happens, William sent along a list of stipulations for a marriage agreement. In case ye succeed in convincing my sister. She might decide Sally is evidence you're not always cold. But mind ye don't think you'll turn things hot with my sister before ye've both tied the knot."

Trent lifted his lantern and studied the fair-haired lad. For one so young, Archie had gumption. And he'd as good as said the Beechams approved his proposal to Edme. Now to convince *her* he wasn't a cold fish.

"Are ye going to hit me?" Archie asked with a saucy grin.

Trent laughed. "Not until after the wedding."

THE NEXT DAY DAWNED GRAY AND CHILLY, AND THE air smelled of snow. Trent went himself to fetch

Sally, Gertrude, and the small bag with the girl's change of clothes.

Whether she'd really heard his short lecture on good behavior, he couldn't be sure. For now, she hopped along, clutching the lead as the dog tugged against it.

"Gertrude doesn't like this rope," Sally said.

"Nevertheless, she must get used to it."

She screwed up her mouth, thinking. "Ah, so when we go into the village, she doesn't run off?"

He smiled down at her. "You won't want Gertrude tugging on you while you're shopping. I have something special planned for her."

They had veered past the gardens and reached the stables. The freckle-faced lad who ran out to greet them was only a few years older than Sally. His face broke in a gap-toothed smile when Gertrude ran over and jumped on him.

"This is her, milord?" He accepted a lick on the cheek and laughed.

"No, Gertrude," Sally said. "Sit."

Gertrude cast a baleful look back and her wiggling bottom almost touched the wet dirt.

"Sally, meet Tom." Tom was Furningwood's youngest stable hand. His stepfather was one of the soldiers Trent had hired, a man who'd looked after the cavalry stable during his military service. "Tom will be giving Gertrude a much-needed bath."

If the dog was dry by nightfall, she could come

sleep in Sally's nursery room. He wouldn't make that promise out loud though.

He would sorely need Edme's help today and that of her maid this night. He'd been greeted at first light with a note from Sir Henry requesting a meeting and sent a reply proposing to meet him in town that morning.

He'd need someone to draw Hatherot's attention so they could speak undisturbed. Not Edme though.

Perhaps Archie might find a way to help him. Despite Edme's warnings that her younger brother had no authority over her, Trent had asked and obtained the lad's permission to court her. In fact, Archie had been well informed of his brother's expectations for a settlement agreement, a secret Archie and William both agreed to conceal from Edme. The terms had been more than he'd expected to promise. But this was Edme, and he'd find a way.

"A bath?" Sally cried. While he was woolgathering, Sally was brewing a temper. "But uncle—"

"I'll look after her, miss." Young Tom kept a grip on Gertrude's lead and laughed as the terrier leapt up again and licked him.

"You can visit Gertrude after we return from the village," Trent said.

Frowning, Sally kicked at the dirt with the toe of her boot.

"Come," he said. "Remember what we talked about? Take my hand."

She raised her gaze to his, nodded, wished Gertude farewell, and placed her small hand in his. At least today, she'd remembered to wear her mittens.

DRESSED IN A WARM WOOLEN GOWN AND PELISSE, AND packed into a fur-lined mantle and muff by Joanie, Edme gathered with the rest of the guests in the hall. The day was gray and only mildly chilly, compared to home. Joanie had sniffed the air and predicted snow, and Edme couldn't disagree. Those who didn't wish to walk the mile to the village might travel by carriage.

While the elder Darnleys settled into a waiting carriage, Mrs. Yardley paced. "I don't know where Cottingwith could be." Her fixed smile didn't reach her eyes, and her color was high, as if she might know what was afoot.

The duke persuaded her to join the Darnleys, and then insisted Hatherot join him and his lady in the next carriage and tell him more about the ore found on his property.

Lady Ottilia begged off from accompanying them, telling her brother she would wait for Lord Cottingwith. A small flame of jealousy flickered in

Edme, but then Lady Ottilia turned her way and winked.

She disliked her brother's company as much as the rest of the guests.

As the carriages pulled out, Cottingwith came around the corner holding Sally's hand.

"Perfect timing," Archie murmured, sending Edme a smile. "Hello, wee poppet," he called, and a grin lit the young girl's face.

Edme came down the steps and greeted Sally.

Archie quickly snatched up the girl's hand. "Come along, Miss Brown," he said, "and I'll make introductions. Ye two catch up with us, if ye can."

She watched as her brother pulled Sally into a circle of cheerful, friendly Darnleys. Lady Ottilia studied the girl, glanced back at Cottingwith and Edme and nodded, and then nudged close to take Sally's other hand.

"Ye told Archie the truth," Edme said.

He lifted her hand and placed it over his arm. "I did. I'm glad you dressed more warmly today."

Laughter spilled from the group in front as they moved down the lane. Archie didn't even look back.

"And ye spoke with him about courting me."

"He brought it up before I could ask his permission. Your brothers love you, Edme Beecham. And so do I."

CHAPTER SEVEN

Fustian. The word sprang to her lips, but she couldn't utter it. Of course, her brothers loved her in their own bossy ways. But Cottingwith—might it be true?

She stopped and rounded on him, opened her mouth, and then closed it, uncertain what to say. Her brother William had insisted she come south—to negotiate with Cottingwith, he said, for terms that would help their business which hadn't fully recovered from the loss of a ship just before her da died.

But there'd been more than one sly innuendo about a match with an English earl. What had William told Archie about a match?

"My brothers love me, ye say. Just what exactly did Archie tell ye to convince ye of that."

Cottingwith glanced to the end of the lane where

the younger people were moving through the gates and out of sight. When he turned back to her, his lips quirked, and he took a deep breath. "I suppose I'll get both your brothers in trouble. Archie told me what William wants in the marriage contract. In great detail." A broad smile revealed one cracked incisor that she'd never noticed before. It detracted not a whit from his looks—quite the opposite in fact.

Yet the smile raised her hackles. Was he so sure of her? And what did he want of her?

There'd been a few sweet words, but he'd mostly talked of his worries about the business and his child.

"Mayhap what ye really want is a better nursemaid," she said flatly, and then felt ashamed. "No. I suppose ye need more help than that, what with your mother stirring mischief. Ye can't send your mam to town?"

"I can, perhaps in a year or two. For now, I'm avoiding the expense of a second household."

Was he tight with the purse strings? No, certainly not. His mother was decked out in the latest of fashions.

London truly was expensive, Filomena said. And keeping two households with two sets of servants would surely drain even a rich man's purse.

He'd taken her hand and started them both off down the road, and then his arm slid around her waist, radiating warmth and evoking a firestorm within her.

"We should catch up," he said. "I'm meeting Sir Henry Rylston in town while the rest of you shop."

"Are ye, indeed," she said infusing her tone with sarcasm.

"He's our local Justice of the Peace. He'll be at dinner tonight, I hope, unless matters develop earlier."

"Matters?"

"Yes. And this is another topic you mustn't discuss with anyone. The excise is tracking a hoy out of Calais bound for the local waters."

"Smuggling? Right in the middle of your house party?"

"I'm afraid so."

"And when do they land?"

"I'll learn more after I talk to him."

She thought of the note slipped into Sally's cottage, the cottage that had been used by the smugglers. "Sally surely must stay in the nursery tonight. Mrs. Ewell as well."

"Mrs. Ewell refused—"

"Is she one of them?"

"Doubtful. She's not from these parts. The families engaged in the trade around here are thick as thieves and don't welcome outsiders."

"Like yourself," she said.

"Or you."

"Or your mother?" Edme shook her head. "There's something funny there with your mother and Taylor. Not amorous, that's not what I'm getting at."

He stopped at the gate, turned her toward him, and leaned under her bonnet. His lips on her were as soft and as cool as the light winter breeze.

"What was that for?"

"For your wisdom. This is your third day here and you've seen that strange alliance."

"Ye've a civil war brewing below stairs, Cottingwith. The butler and the housekeeper are at odds. The housemaids perform well enough, and the footmen—"

"Yes. You're right. Come, let's catch up."

He waved to the others who paused and waited for Edme and Cottingwith.

EDME STOOD OUTSIDE THE MERCANTILE STORE WITH Lady Ottilia while the Darnley girls had Sally help them pick out ribbons and Filomena supervised all three. Edme had helped the lass budget her five pence among candy and small toys. She'd seen in the girl's shining eyes the doll she admired.

"What fun she's having," Lady Ottilia said. "I suppose she's not allowed into town often, poor mite. What a pity fivepence wouldn't purchase that doll."

Edme drew the other woman away from the door. "As soon as she steps out, I'll return and order it for her. But, *shh*, don't ye say a word."

A wistful smile lurked on the other woman's lips. "Best check with her... er, Cottingwith. He might have already purchased it." She squeezed Edme's hand. "To see a child's shining eyes. It's magic."

Tears glistened in the taller woman's eyes.

"Aye, 'tis true. Ye must marry and have a few babes of your own to spoil, Lady Ottilia." She averted her gaze and saw Cottingwith on the other side of the High Street with another man.

Lady Ottilia's gaze followed hers and she drew in a sharp breath. Cottingwith and the other man saw them and crossed the street to join them.

"Miss Edme Beecham, Lady Ottilia, may I introduce Sir Henry Rylston. Sir Henry, the ladies are our guests for the Yuletide."

If she'd turned away an instant earlier, she'd have missed Sir Henry's look of shock, and the slightest of flushes in his cheeks. Beside her, Lady Ottilia had stiffened, and a bland mask had dropped hiding her previous emotions.

"Sir Henry served as a diplomat abroad and has retired to Kent," Cottingwith said. "He is my near neighbor and a great friend, and he's promised to join us for dinner tonight."

"Lady Ottilia and I have met before," Sir Henry

said. "I hope we may have a few moments to, er reminisce, tonight, my lady."

She inclined her head, regally, and Edme swore she was pressing her lips to hide trembling.

Oh ho. There was more here than a mere acquaintance. Did Cottingwith see it as well?

She glanced at him, but he'd fallen back into his usual unreadable expression.

Sir Henry dipped his head. "I must be off. I'll see all of you tonight."

"Excuse me," Lady Ottilia said, and slipped into the store.

"They know each other," Edme said.

"As he told us. How is Sally's shopping faring?"

She sighed. Cottingwith was a man. He'd entirely missed the tension between Sir Henry and Lady Ottilia.

"Quite well. She finally accepted that she could only purchase five peppermint sticks and a game of jacks. And then she began to wheedle the rest of us, but so sweetly that no one could do aught but laugh."

"I see." He shook his head. "Where are your brother and the other men?"

"In the tavern, drinking." Pouring brandy and ale down Hatherton's gullet was the way Archie put it. She'd likely have to pour her brother into his bed for a nap.

"And my mother?"

"A footman came running with a message, and she and Lord and Lady Darnley returned."

He swore quietly.

"Before ye hare off after her, ye must tell me this —have ye bought your lass the yellow haired doll perched there in the window?"

"Dolls," he breathed out. "No, Edme Beecham." He moved in closer, smelling of the brandy he must have shared with Sir Henry. "I've been preoccupied with other things."

"More important things?"

"No. Different things. And in any case, I bought her a doll for her birthday."

"The brown-haired doll." Edme gasped. "I've forgotten to tell ye. Ye've a footman named Herbert who told Sally the doll ye gave her was ugly and so was she."

Fire flared in his eyes before he dropped a shade over it.

"He's some relation to Taylor, my maid says. I didn't have a chance to ask Sally where she ran into him."

"I suppose we know who delivered that note," he said finally.

The others spilled out the door, laughing, and he took a step back. Sally ran to him, her face glowing, her small purchases in hand.

Cottingwith crouched down to inspect them and commend her, and then sent her and the others off to the confectionary shop next door with more coins.

Edme stood fast. He turned a smile on her, took her hand and drew her into the store.

* * *

THE WEE MARQUESS OF LITHGOW LAUGHED, GURGLED, and squealed, toddling, crawling, and rolling with Sally Brown on the nursery floor carpet while Edme, Joanie, and Morag, Lithgow's nursemaid watched.

"Naughty Sally might be," Joanie murmured, "but at heart a good lass. Ye'll do right by her, Miss Edme."

Morag sent her a curious smile, and she felt her cheeks warming.

A scrabbling noise at the door saved her from more of Joanie's speculation. Sally set Lithgow aside and jumped up just as Gertrude bounded into the room towing a young boy by her lead.

Sally wrapped the dog in a fierce hug. Gertrude jumped free and went for the babe.

As Sally bent to intervene, Edme held her breath, but bursting with giggles, Lithgow plopped down on the floor and accepted the licking and sniffing.

His nursemaid watched. "Not afraid of the dogs, is our wee lordship," she said.

"Here she is, Miss Sally," the young boy said. "All clean."

"Did ye bathe her yourself, Tom?" Edme asked the boy.

"Yes, milady. About gave me a bath too with her shaking."

"I want to help you next time," Sally said, rising. Gertrude made her way to the low table where the remains of a luncheon lay.

"I did feed her," the boy said.

"Oh, Gertrude is always hungry." Sally reached for his hand and tugged him. "This is Lord Lithgow. Do you want to play with us?"

A masculine throat clearing drew their attention to the door, where a footman stood. Most footmen kept their faces expressionless. This one glared at the boy.

No. His wrathful gaze focused on Sally. All the joy had fled from her little face, and she glared back, her lower lip trembling.

Edme stepped into their line of sight and turned to the footman. Tall, handsome, and dark-haired under his half-wig, she must have seen him before, but she'd grown attuned to the aristocratic way of not noticing servants.

She could guess who he was.

"Step into the corridor, Herbert," she said. "I'll have a word with ye."

His eyes flashed anger. "I'm to escort the boy back to the stables."

"I'll see he makes his way back without lifting the silver."

"I don't answer to your kind. Mr. Taylor expressly said—"

A shadow appeared in the corridor. "Said what, Herbert?"

Cottingwith's tone was deceptively calm, but when the stunned footman moved out of her way, Edme saw the fury under the fixed expression. There was more passion in the man than she'd realized. She followed the servant out and closed the nursery door.

The air in the passage fairly crackled with masculine ire, the heat of upcoming battle. Evenly matched in height and shoulders the men were, but she'd put her money on Cottingwith's strength of will.

After a long moment, the footman blinked. "I'm to escort the stable lad downstairs immediately."

"Miss Beecham is an honored guest," Cottingwith said. "Apologize at once."

Mouth pressed into a firm line, the younger man bowed to her and mumbled an apology.

That it hadn't been good enough for Cottingwith, she could tell by the set of his jaw.

"Report to my study in fifteen minutes."

Herbert's face hardened into an angry mask, and he left.

"Will ye dismiss him?" she whispered.

Cottingwith framed her face with his hands. "I'm sorry he treated you badly."

"He may pack up and leave on his own."

He nodded and pressed his lips to hers, a brief press that nevertheless set her heart thumping. And then while her heart leapt into a somersault, he kissed her forehead and stepped back.

The passion was apparently all on her side.

"I must have a moment with Sally," he said.

Edme followed him into the nursery where the children and the baby rolled about on the floor, the dog feinting and bounding while trying to lick them.

Perhaps Tom might be a playmate for Sally.

* * *

DINNER THAT NIGHT HAD BEEN A GRAND AFFAIR WITH additional guests and several removes of multiple dishes. Mrs. Yardley's plans for a long stint in the drawing room thereafter were disrupted by the weather. The snow that had been threatening began to fall just before ten, and most of the local families made their apologies and departed.

The gentlemen disappeared to the billiards room, Lady Ottilia stepped away to retrieve a shawl and never returned, and Mrs. Darnley, claiming fatigue, shepherded her two girls upstairs. Not wishing to be left alone with Mrs. Yardley, Edme followed Filomena up to the nursery.

"I noticed our hostess glaring at you," Filomena said.

Edme hadn't had a private moment to speak to the duchess. Nor in fact had she been able to find out what Cottingwith had done about Herbert, but she hadn't seen the footman since.

"Ye can look at Sally and see what this is about," Edme said. "But I'll tell ye all after we tuck in the wee ones."

Half an hour later they were seated in Edme's private parlor in front of a crackling fire, sipping sherry. Joanie had popped in and gone through to lay out Edme's night clothes before returning to the nursery.

"I declare," Filomena said. "The aura in Furningwood is anything but restful. Aside from Cottingwith's dragon of a mother, did you notice the strained looks between Lady Ottilia and the neighbor, Sir Henry Rylston?"

On the closer examination allowed when they gathered for dinner, she saw that the balding middle-aged baronet stood barely of a height with Lady Ottilia, and he was more of a scholarly sort than a braw man.

"There's something between them, though if ever a couple was mismatched it's them," Edme said.

Rather like herself and Cottingwith.

Oh now, that was a thought. Mayhap both men had deeper reservoirs of passion than one might

117

think. She shook herself. "They went off together into a corner. Hatherot looked puzzled about that at first, and then he began to glare, and I thought he would interrupt except your duke had him cornered and wouldn't stop talking."

"Andrew is quite the promoter. He was no doubt crowing about the stag hunt last month. I wonder how close brother and sister are."

"Perhaps not very close," Edme said. "Perhaps I've misjudged her."

Filomena drained her glass and poured another. "Perhaps. Now, what did you wish to speak about. I'm at my leisure. Andrew is off with our host doing God knows what and he told me not to wait up for him."

"I wonder if Archie is in the billiards room with the Darnleys and Hatherot."

Filomena wrinkled her nose. "Hatherot," she said. "Ugh. Now, enough dodging. Are you going to tell me about Cottingwith and his daughter?"

Edme choked as she swallowed.

"Sally *is* his daughter, isn't she?"

"Yes. There's a story there. He hasn't said whether or not I may share it, so I won't, not entirely, except to say he's been supporting her since her birth and didn't know she was his until last Christmas."

"When he left Kinmarty."

"Aye."

"And as she's just arrived in the nursery here—"

"She's been living in a cottage on the grounds with a lady he hired to look after her."

Filomena's face froze in a frown, and then she nodded. "His mother, I presume, objects? What do *you* say, Edme?"

Edme squeezed her friend's hand. "Ye know what I say. I say, born on the right or the wrong side of the blanket, a child belongs with his or her family."

"Why did he wait until now to bring her up to the manor? To embarrass his high-in-the-instep mother?" She flashed a wry look. "*Ah.* Men. He did it because you're here now."

"No." She shook her head. Cottingwith was a caring man. "Something happened two days ago and..." Dare she tell Filomena about the smuggling? Not yet.

But she told her the story about meeting the girl on her morning walk with Cottingwith, about the note from Father Christmas and the gift left in the shed for the lass.

"So, the Father Christmas story she shared with us was not just her imagination. Who would do such a thing?"

"The cottage was used by the local smugglers to store contraband, with a wink and a nod from the previous earl. Cottingwith has been discouraging the free traders, and it's possible the harassment may have come from one of them."

"I wonder..." Filomena went to the bedchamber door and called for Joanie.

The maid appeared.

"What is it, Filomena?" Edme asked.

Filomena frowned and straightened. "Joanie, you were to stay in the nursery tonight, weren't you? Yet I know you must be tired, as is Morag. The tension in this house... Something is afoot. Evan will sleep in my bedchamber tonight, and I dare say you have room for Sally here as well. The nursery here is too drafty anyway, Morag says."

Edme expelled a long breath and stood. "Sally was feigning sleep, I believe. And I sensed she was nervous in the new surroundings, especially without Gertrude." Tom had taken the dog back to the stables with him. "Let's fetch them both."

"I'll go, miss," Joanie said. "And we'll have the nursery maid carry his little lordship down."

Filomena stood. "We'll all go."

They met the housekeeper, Mrs. Hunnycrest, on her way to the nursery. When they told her their plan, a look of relief crossed her face. "I thought to come and see whether anything else was needed in the nursery," she said.

"What's afoot?" Edme asked.

"I don't know. His lordship went out with Mr. Beecham, the duke, and Sir Henry."

"And Lord Hatherot?" Edme asked.

The housekeeper frowned. "I saw him in the

passage near my lord's bedchamber, and again later entering his sister's room."

"And what of the Darnleys?"

"His lordship and her ladyship had strong tisanes sent up when they retired. The young ladies are in bed, as far as I know. The young gentlemen are in the billiards room at the far end of the manor. I just brought them another bottle of brandy so…"

"So, you'll find them stretched on the billiards table in the morn," Filomena said, then exchanged a look with Edme. "But *you* fetched them the bottle, Mrs. Hunnycrest?"

Not the butler, who would have the key to the liquor cabinet.

The housekeeper merely nodded.

While most of the other servants had retired for the night, Mrs. Hunnycrest had been roaming the halls of Furningwood doing Taylor's work, when she ought to be in her bed sleeping. Strange.

FILOMENA GATHERED UP HER SLEEPING BABE, AND Edme ushered Sally into her dressing gown.

"We'll return to your parlor, Edme," Filomena said. "Until the men return." She sent the housekeeper and Lithgow's nursemaid, Morag, to move a cot to her bedchamber. Joanie went off to fetch a tea tray.

They settled the baby into Edme's bed and

stacked pillows between him and the edge of the bed. Sally climbed into the bed next to him, and Edme dropped a kiss on her forehead. "There now, we'll be right through that door in the next room, and then when the wee one leaves, we'll disassemble his pillow fort, and I'll take his place."

Sally clutched her hand. "What will happen to me?"

Edme's heart twisted. There was real fear in the child's voice.

And rightly so. She'd been bandied about for these first years of her life.

"Ye'll live in Furningwood Manor and grow up here. Lord Cottingwith will take care of ye. He'll hire a nursery staff who'll look after ye, and a governess who'll teach ye to be a young lady."

"His mother doesn't like me."

What was she to say to that?

"You're important to him, Sally Brown, and he's the master of Furningwood. Mind ye, he'll expect good behavior, and when ye're naughty he'll punish ye, so ye know how to go on in the world. Don't ye fret about who likes ye and who doesn't."

Lord Lithgow chose that moment to shake his arms and emit a croak.

Sally smiled. "I wish he was my brother. The duchess is nice," she said. "And the duke. And Mr. Archie. He pulls my hair and makes me laugh. My uncle—I don't always think he likes me."

Ach. "My brother, Archie is a scamp," Edme said. "Lord Cottingwith, on the other hand, is what ye call 'reserved'. But he cares for ye, darling girl. Never doubt it."

Tears licked the corners of her own eyes. 'Twas a lesson she might heed herself.

She forced a smile, pulled the yawning girl into a hug, told her to go sleep, and returned to the parlor.

Before Edme reached her chair, a knock came at the door, and she went to answer it. Lady Ottilia slipped in silently.

"Your grace," she said, halting and letting out a breath.

"Come and sit yourself down. My maid is bringing tea." The door opened. "And here she is. Joanie, we'll need another cup." Edme spotted the empty sherry. "And fetch more sherry from Archie's room."

"Sherry's gone. There might be whisky though."

"Or check our room," Filomena said.

When the door closed, Lady Ottilia cleared her throat. "I... well, I'm glad to see the both of you here. I know it's late but, but... I wanted to ask for your help."

"It's a night for helping lasses in distress," Filomena said. "What may Edme and I do for *you*?"

"You're already giving me refuge. Hatherot was making his way to my bedchamber, planning to plague me."

The skin on Edme's neck crawled. "The housekeeper saw him enter your room." She shared a glance with Filomena.

"Don't misunderstand," Lady Ottilia said. "He's not... not after my person. Nor is he after money. God knows I have little of that. He's angry with me. He wants me to chase Cottingwith and I won't do it. And... he's worked out that Sir Henry..." She squeezed her eyes shut for a long moment. "I ought to start at the beginning and pray that both of you can keep a confidence."

Edme nodded, still unsure whether to give the woman her full trust. But keeping secrets, that she could do. "I can, Lady Ottilia, and I will."

"As will I," Filomena said.

CHAPTER EIGHT

Tears filled the other woman's eyes as she told her story. Three years earlier, she'd met Sir Henry in Paris. They'd had an affair, one that Sir Henry ended when his wife left her French lover and returned to him. Then Lady Ottilia escaped to England and discovered that she was increasing. She journeyed north to a private cottage, distraught and alone but for her old, trusted maid, and lost her baby late in the pregnancy.

Hatherot had wheedled the story out of a servant later. He didn't know who the father was, but he vowed to search out the culprit who had made his sister more difficult to marry off.

"When Mrs. Yardley's invitation to this party arrived, I jumped at the chance I might see Sir Henry again. His wife died last year, you see. I knew he'd settled near here. I hoped he might be invited here, and if not, that I might find the courage to call on him, to tell him."

"He didn't know?" Edme asked.

"At first, I was too angry to tell him, and then I was crushed by... by what I'd done. And then when our son came early and died." She shook her head. "I wanted to die as well."

Edme reached for Lady Ottilia's hand. "How may we help you?"

Before Lady Ottilia could reply, Joanie entered and set a bottle of Kinmarty whisky on the table. "All I could find," she said. "From your husband's valet, your grace."

A baby's cry came from the bedchamber.

"I'll just check on him." Filomena went through to the bedroom with Joanie following.

Lady Ottilia turned to Edme. "I'm leaving tomorrow. Sir Henry will come for me in his carriage. He has a cousin in residence who will chaperone us until he can fetch a special license. I just need to dodge my brother and my maid. I think she's been spying for him. I wasn't able to pack—"

"We'll send your things on to Sir Henry's," Edme said. "Cottingwith can arrange it."

"I hope so. Try as I might, I haven't been able to drum up the courage to ask for his help. I saw him talking with Sir Henry quite intently tonight. I hope he won't interfere with our plans or tell my brother."

"I believe the earl is no friend to your brother," Edme said.

Filomena returned without Joanie and sat down. "Joanie told me the valet said Andrew has come back and will be along momentarily."

At a knock at the door, Edme jumped up and admitted the Duke of Kinmarty. His hair glistened with dampness, and his boots were wet.

"What's happened?" she asked.

He spotted Lady Ottilia and shook his head. "Is all well here?"

"I've brought Evan down from the nursery," Filomena said, rising. "He's in Edme's bed for now. Sally is with him. Come, let's check on them."

They went into the bedchamber and then Filomena returned alone. "He left through the bedroom's door to the corridor," she said.

TEMPER RISING, MERTICE YARDLEY PEEKED INTO THE dark drawing room and went along to the billiards room where only the two Darnley boys were playing, drunkenly unkempt and slurring their words. Still, they were able to convey that the marquess had left some time ago. No, Cottingwith had not joined them, nor the duke, nor Beecham. Father and Mother had retired for the night, they said, as had their sisters.

The marquess was a thorn in Mertice's side. It

wasn't her fault she'd not yet been able to push her stubborn son into a marriage with Lady Ottilia.

She tried the door to the study, found it locked, and went out to the terrace and peered into the dark room. Cottingwith wouldn't be sitting in darkness.

Where could he be? He'd foisted that child upon her houseguests. Installed her in the nursery with the son of a duke. He'd invited the Justice of the Peace to dinner without her knowledge on a night when...

"Keep still, mother," Cottingwith had said when she'd complained about Rylston. "You're lucky I didn't invite the Riding Officer."

Did he know? She must speak with her foolish son this very night.

He'd dodged her after dinner, and her guests, *all* of her guests, had dispersed like pins in a game of bowls.

Nor could she find Taylor, but that was not surprising with so much afoot. He'd be busy with messages and orders.

Her maid had seen Taylor that afternoon speaking with Hatherot, but they'd gone silent before she could eavesdrop. Mertice had cornered the butler later, and in his usual way he'd cajoled her to trust him, that her share of the profits would be substantial, that he would never do anything to harm her or the earl.

He hadn't mentioned the child, and there'd been

no time to question him about that business with the mouse. She didn't want the brat at Furningwood, not even in that old cottage where the men had stored their goods before her son became earl. But the mouse... she'd have the truth out of Taylor before this was finished.

She'd set Cottingwith straight as well. He'd refused to listen to all her warnings. He'd refused to be guided by her, when she'd been the one standing between him and the ire of the local people he'd hurt, the people whose only crime had been the industry his uncle and cousin had protected. Her foolish, foolish son. If the child should be hurt, it would be Cottingwith's fault for not heeding her guidance.

Returning inside, she woke the sleepy-eyed footman serving as night porter. He'd seen none of the gents, except for Lord Hatherot, who'd been looking for Lady Ottilia.

They must all be upstairs in their bedchambers. She'd run Cottingwith to earth there.

When she knocked on her son's bedchamber door, no one answered. She pushed the door open. A lamp burned dimly, but the room was empty. The coats Cottingwith wore at dinner hung over a chair. He'd changed out of his formal evening wear sometime after his valet had retired to his quarters upstairs.

Surely, Cottingwith wasn't going out this night?

Taylor would have told her if her son had left the manor.

Or... might he be visiting someone's bedchamber?

A sickening suspicion came over her. That impertinent Mrs. Hunnycrest had placed that Scottish trollop in the green suite, the best suite in the north wing, at Cottingwith's orders, she'd claimed.

Her son was there, visiting the red-haired harlot.

She with her fine silks and laces—well what would one expect of the chit. Of course, she'd have access to fine goods. Her people bought and sold cloth. But most tradesmen had the good sense not to set their daughters up to ape their betters.

Mertice moved silently along in the dim light of the wing housing Cottingwith, and just as she reached the balcony overlooking the entry hall, in the distance she saw a dark-haired man turn down the passage of the north wing. He reached the door of the green suite, knocked, and was admitted.

Caught in the act. She'd send Edme Beecham packing that very night.

She picked her way carefully in the darkness, taking her time. Let her find them in *flagrante delicto*; oh yes. When she reached the door, she heard footfalls inside, the creaking of hinges and an interior door snicking shut.

Headed into the bedroom, they were. She paused

a moment and considered entering through the door that opened from the passage into the bedchamber. Odds were, that would be locked and rattling the door would alert them. No. She'd wait in the private sitting room a few moments and then spring her surprise.

Without knocking, she turned the knob and entered.

Three sets of eyes turned shocked looks on her, and the anger spurring her swelled into livid indignation. Miss Edme Beecham, a nobody, sat perched in a Chippendale chair in this exquisite room, hosting her own entertainment. The duchess stood by the closed bedroom door, her hand on the knob, and of all people, Lady Ottilia perched on the edge of a settee.

Blood pounded in her ears. She, Mrs. Mertice Yardley, who ought to have been a countess—she was the hostess, not this upstart holding court in the bedchamber she'd meant to assign to the marquess's sister.

Pah, but look at her guest, the duchess. She was no better than she should be. She was an upstart, like Miss Beecham.

But Lady Ottilia? She was from one of the oldest families in England.

"Ma'am." The red-haired tart rose from her seat, something she hadn't had the courtesy to do the previous afternoon. "Is something the matter?"

* * *

FEAR RIPPLED THROUGH EDME. SHE SURMISED IT WAS hot anger suffusing Mrs. Yardley's broad face, but as that lady's gaze turned toward the bedchamber, the color in her cheeks drained.

"Is something the matter?" Edme repeated.

Visions flashed. Perhaps after the duke left Cottingwith, something had happened to him.

"I'm looking for Cottingwith," Mrs. Yardley said, her voice so tight, Edme could feel the hostility rippling.

So, it wasn't concern for her son driving their hostess.

"And you thought Cottingwith would be here?" Filomena asked, a note of haughtiness in her voice. "You can see he is not."

Color rose again in the older woman's cheeks, but she held her ground. "He's not in his bedchamber or anywhere in the manor, and..." She bit down on her lip.

"Ye thought he would be visiting my bed." Edme said. "Ye may go have a look if ye wish, but ye'll find that at present, there's a marquess occupying that place."

Mrs. Yardley blinked and sent an astonished glance Lady Ottilia's way.

Edme squashed a smile. The joke had been

almost too easy. "Go through then, but please don't disturb him."

The blinking accelerated, and a touch of remorse rose in Edme. This was Cottingwith's mother. Fear was ruling her, he'd said.

But fear of what? She had everything: a home, fine clothes, and a good son.

If she married Cottingwith, she'd have to put up with the woman. She'd best try to be civil.

"Don't misunderstand me, ma'am," Edme said. "The marquess in my bed is Lithgow, not Hatherot. I've no idea where Lady Ottilia's brother is."

The mention of Lady Ottilia snapped Cottingwith's mother out of her spell. "Your brother was looking for you, Lady Ottilia," the lady said. "I'm surprised to find you here."

"When I retired, I found I wasn't at all sleepy," Lady Ottilia said smoothly, "and I was on my way to the, er, library to look for a book when I encountered her grace in the passage, and she invited me along."

The bit about not being sleepy was undoubtedly true, but Lady Ottilia had stumbled so badly over the lie that Edme found she liked Hatherot's sister better and better.

A scratching noise sent Edme to the door.

She turned the knob and fear jolted through her, freezing her in place a long moment. The haughty butler entered, fully dressed in the dark coats and trousers he'd worn all through the evening.

As her nerves settled, she pondered the fact that the housekeeper and butler were both roaming the corridors of Furningwood, long past the hour when busy servants might expect to retire.

"Taylor." Mrs. Yardley's tone held a reprimand.

Taylor scanned the room with a frankness unusual to English servants, especially when a duchess was present. The look had been almost calculating. He opened his mouth, then pressed his thin lips together as if thinking better of what he'd planned to say.

"A word, madame," he said, finally. It was a demand, not a question, and it sent Mrs. Yardley's back up an inch.

The butler eyed his mistress with equal haughtiness. "About the matter you wanted to discuss?"

His tone dripped with contempt. Edme scanned him up and down again and noticed he wore boots, and they were muddy.

Taylor. Taylor was involved in the smuggling. He was also likely behind Herbert's intimidation of Sally. What about Mrs. Hunnycrest? Was she involved as well?

Was Mrs. Yardley? Perhaps that was the root of the lady's fear—she might get caught.

The thought sent hot anger through Edme. For a

good price on brandy or silk she was risking her son's reputation, all while looking down her long nose at the Beechams. If she were to be arrested... how terrible that would be for Cottingwith. He might be implicated, if not by the authorities, then by a whispering campaign of slander. For certain, his business would suffer.

"Never mind," Mrs. Yardley said. "You may retire. I won't need you anymore tonight."

Think quickly lass. She must try to keep both these scallywags here. Perhaps she could send Fil after the duke.

"A moment, Taylor." Edme exchanged a look with Fil. "Where is Cottingwith? His mother was seeking him. For that matter, where is Hatherot?"

Anger glinted in his eyes, raising her hackles. The fireplace poker was within Lady Ottilia's reach, though she wasn't sure she could rely on the woman to come to her aid with it.

"Where is Cottingwith?" Edme fought to keep her voice level. "Have ye done something to him?"

Mrs. Yardley gasped, but Edme couldn't look away from the looming man.

"I don't answer to your sort," the butler said.

Hades. She fought not to flinch. She'd never be able to keep the man here against his will tonight.

Edme managed a tight smile and nodded. "Your nephew, Herbert, said the same thing. I'll remember ye both said that, Taylor."

After one final defiant glare, Taylor withdrew, closing the door softly. Edme stepped to the fireplace and fetched a poker. "Your man needs a crack in the head, Mrs. Yardley. Before he's packed off from Furningwood."

Mrs. Yardley glanced at her as if she was the lowliest beetle who'd just crawled from under the floorboard.

If she was the Countess of Cottingwith, she'd send this piece of baggage off to a cottage in the Outer Hebrides.

Filomena moved closer and set her arm around Edme's shoulder. "He *was* very rude, Mrs. Yardley."

"Extremely insolent," Lady Ottilia said. "This is a very strange sort of house party."

Their hostess's eyes widened, mayhap with visions of social calamity. "I shall speak with him. Do not the rest of you wish to retire? And your child, your grace. Surely, you'll want him to sleep in the nursery."

"I think not," Filomena said. "I'll feel much better having him near after hearing about the trick played on poor little Sally. As well as this scene with your butler."

"But…" Mrs. Yardley's eyes narrowed. "That had nothing to do with the servants here. That child is a charity case that—"

"Careful, ma'am," Edme said gently. "We all know what that child is to Cottingwith. Well, perhaps not

Lady Ottilia. But I don't believe she's so high in the instep as to treat the lass unkindly."

Lady Ottilia blinked. "No indeed. But what trick was played on her?"

"Someone sent her a note saying that Father Christmas had left an early gift for her in the garden shed. The gift was—"

"I'd thank you to not spread that story," Mrs. Yardley said with a wild-eyed glance at Lady Ottilia.

"A gift-wrapped dead mouse," Edme said. "Fortunately, Cottingwith and I encountered her before she could go looking into the shed."

A scratch at the door brought the housekeeper again.

"What is it now, Hunnycrest?" Mrs. Yardley asked.

"Sir Henry is downstairs, looking for Taylor. Says it's urgent."

Mrs. Yardley's face turned a stark shade of white, and her lips purpled like Edme's father's had done with his last attack before his death.

"Sit, Mrs. Yardley," Edme said, steering the woman to a chair. "Someone fetch her some spirits. I'll go down and speak to the man."

Resisting, the older lady staggered and leaned against the wall.

Lady Ottilia jumped up. "I'm going as well."

Mrs. Yardley downed the drink Filomena handed her and straightened. "No. I'm mistress of

Furningwood, not you. I'll go down, and you'll stay here."

Edme exchanged a look with Lady Ottilia and marched to the door, still clutching the poker.

"Joanie and I will see to things here," Filomena called. "Come back and tell me what's happened."

"Lock all the doors," Edme called.

The angry muttering and pant of Mrs. Yardley pursued them down the stairs.

WHEN THEY REACHED THE PARLOR, MRS. YARDLEY pushed past them and squared up on her visitor, still catching her breath. "What can this be about, Sir Henry?" she asked finally, when she could speak.

"Mrs. Yardley." He dipped his head, greeted Edme, and went to clasp Lady Ottilia's hand. "A slight delay, my dear," he told her. Edme was close enough to hear his whisper.

"Sir Henry?" Mrs. Yardley prompted.

"I'd hoped to speak with Lord Cottingwith," he said affably.

"He's not here."

Sir Henry raised an eyebrow. "Not yet? Well, he'll be along shortly. Where is your butler, Taylor?"

"He's not here either. He's… I believe he's gone to look for my son."

Edme stepped up. "We just saw Taylor a few

moments ago. All of us. Mrs. Yardley, where did he go?"

Cottingwith's mother spluttered. "Why you..."

Her face turned an ugly shade of purple.

"Do sit down, madam." Sir Henry's voice held genuine concern. Leading her to a sofa, he all but pushed her down, and then signaled. Two men emerged from the shadows of the poorly lit room. "Our men outside the house haven't seen Taylor leave. I'm afraid they'll need to search the house for him. Mrs. Hunnycrest, we'll start below stairs, if you would kindly show them the way."

The housekeeper, who'd been lurking behind them, led the two men off.

Mrs. Yardley's hands curled into fists. "How dare you search Furningwood. I didn't give my permission."

"Your son did, madam, earlier tonight. Captain Davis and his men in the coastal patrol have stopped a hoy loaded with some rather fine contraband, and they pointed to Furningwood as the place they were bringing the goods. I should like to speak with *you* while we wait for Cottingwith's arrival. Ladies, if you would return to your bedchambers, I can have one of my men escort you. Though I see, Miss Beecham, that you've armed yourself already."

Edme rolled the poker in her hands. Thank God they'd brought the children down from the nursery. Taylor could be anywhere in the manor.

Most likely though, she reminded herself, he'd gone out a door or a window and slipped past the watchers outside.

"We'll return and join the duchess in my sitting room," Edme said. "When Cottingwith is free, would ye ask him to come speak with, er, us?"

"Yes. It shouldn't be long."

Kinmarty stalked in and greeted them, and then took Sir Henry off into a corner for a whispered conversation. He'd changed out of his damp coat and boots.

Mrs. Yardley tried to push herself up. Sir Henry hurried over and offered her a flask which she waved away.

"She'll make herself ill," Lady Ottilia whispered.

"Aye." Perhaps illness would be a way for Cottingwith to smooth over his mother's crimes, for surely, she was somehow involved with Taylor.

"I'll escort you ladies," Kinmarty said, rejoining them.

"Nay," Edme said. "Mrs. Yardley believes her man has left the manor. With Sir Henry's men around, we should be fine. B-but..." She took in a breath trying to still her shaking voice. "Where is Cottingwith? Where is Archie?"

The duke patted her shoulder. "I'm certain they'll be right along. When they arrive, we'll come immediately. Hurry along now and use that poker if you need to. If all else fails, scream."

With Mrs. Yardley sputtering objections, Kinmarty went to offer his own flask and Sir Henry pulled Lady Ottilia aside for a brief whispered conversation. Then both ladies slipped out of the parlor into the frigid hall.

CHAPTER NINE

"Goodness." Lady Ottilia pulled her shawl tight. "Mrs. Yardley certainly knows how to throw an interesting house party. Is Cottingwith a smuggler?"

Edme shook her head and moved to the stairs. She prayed he was safe. The blasted man had told her next to nothing about his plans for this night.

"His butler then?" Lady Ottilia stuck close to her, and they ascended together.

"It would seem so," Edme said. "I don't know for certain."

Lady Ottilia gasped. "His *mother*. Oh. Poor Cottingwith—an illegitimate child and a mother who's a criminal."

They'd reached the top of the stairs and nerves skittering, Edme rounded on her companion. "I never said that about his mother, and I'd thank ye to not spread that story."

"No." Lady Ottilia gripped her hand. "Forgive me. I have my own scandal to conceal. I only hope... Sir Henry promises he'll take me away tonight when he's finished his assignment. He wants me to pack. Will you come with me? It's impossible to trust my maid."

And Edme wondered again if she should trust Lady Ottilia. Plus, they were supposed to check on the others.

Filomena had Joanie, and Joanie would fight to the death for the bairns.

"Yes. But we'll throw everything together quickly and we'll repack when we reach my rooms."

* * *

"ALL IN ALL, A GOOD NIGHT'S WORK," CAPTAIN DAVIS said. "Despite not apprehending the local crew."

The hoy's French captain and crew had been seized with the boat and the cargo of brandy, gin, and textiles.

"Thank you for your help, Lord Cottingwith, Mr. Beecham, Mr. Jelson."

His ship works partner, Jelson had joined them, prepared to convey the ringleader to a ship destined for the antipodes waiting at the Nore.

Not that they'd told Davis about that plan.

Archie grinned, mounting his horse. "Happy to take those goods out of competition for Beecham Trading. We pay our duties."

Trent mounted and they picked their way back to the manor, worry nagging at him.

"We almost had them," Archie said. "I've never seen men scatter like beetles before."

"In truth, I'm glad, Archie. I'd hate to see any of my tenants arrested. The man in charge though…"

"I wish Edme had been along to meet you, Jelson." Archie laughed. "Though, on second thought, I'm glad she's safe and snug in her bed at the manor."

"I'll meet her at breakfast," Jelson said. "Then, unless we find your man, I'll be off. Either way, my wife, Rose will want me home for Christmas."

Trent hoped Edme was safe and snug, and he hoped they'd find Taylor.

Sir Henry had men surrounding the house. When there was no sign of Taylor, Sir Henry and the duke returned to Furningwood to smoke him out while Cottingwith and the others assisted the officers in the futile effort of trying to round up the locals.

Letting Archie and Jelson chatter on, Trent kept his own counsel and pushed his mount as quickly as the snowy roads would allow.

When they arrived at Furningwood, and entered through the kitchens, they found Mrs. Hunnycrest in the servants hall waiting to lead Sir Henry's men through the larder and laundry room.

"What's afoot?" Trent asked her.

"Sir Henry has them searching the house for Taylor," she said. "Sir Henry is in the drawing room with Mrs. Yardley and the duke. The others are in the bedchambers, 'cept for the two young gentlemen. They were in the billiards room last I saw them."

"The servants?"

"James is serving as night porter. The rest have gone to bed."

"We'll stay and help with the search," Jelson said. "What say you, Beecham?"

* * *

Minutes later, Trent heard his mother's indignant voice from the drawing room. "I know nothing about any smuggling."

She spotted him as soon as he entered the drawing room and cast him a glare.

"Here is Cottingwith. Ask him your impertinent questions."

Sir Henry lifted an eyebrow. The duke turned back to the sideboard where he was pouring a drink.

The questioning was a farce, for the benefit of Sir Henry's superiors. They all knew it, except for Mother of course, but she was playing the role of incensed matron perfectly, as he knew she would.

"My apologies, Sir Henry. Despite her rudeness, my mother is right. You'd best put your questions to me."

"*Rude*," she said, shooting to her feet. "The man has dinner at my house and then a few hours later he has the gall to search it."

"*My* house, Mother, and with my permission."

"I suppose it's awkward," Sir Henry said, "with a house party in progress. Lady Ottilia and Miss Beecham have just returned upstairs. Perhaps we should check on them and escort your mother to her rooms. You might wish to lock yourself in, madam, until we find Taylor."

"Taylor has done nothing wrong," she said.

"Then he won't mind me questioning him."

"Come, Mother." Trent reached for her, and she cringed away.

A scream pierced the silence. He ran for the stairs.

* * *

EDME AND LADY OTTILIA TURNED AT THE LANDING and hurried down the passage to the south wing.

"Are ye sure Sir Henry will marry ye?" Edme asked. "I'm sure Cottingwith would allow ye to stay here... Oh, but what a quandary is here."

"Yes. A quandary and my brother."

They reached Lady Ottilia's bedchamber and

found the door locked. Lady Ottilia looked up, confused. "What…"

The door opened with a jolt, and Lady Ottilia all but fell into the room. A pair of strong hands reached for Edme as well, wrenching her inside.

The bedside lamp flickered, illuminating a body. Hatherot lay there, eyes shut, breathing heavily. A maid huddled on the floor next to him. And the black figure behind the hands slithered out of the shadows and slammed the door before Edme could get over the shock.

Sally's tormentor, Herbert, was here.

Edme turned sideways, the poker hidden in the folds of her skirts.

"What have you done to my brother?" Lady Ottilia walked to the bed, and the maid scooted aside. "Get up off the floor, Birdie. What the deuce have you done?"

The maid struggled up, sobbing.

"Stop that," Lady Ottilia said. "Why is Hatherot here?" She sent Herbert a glare. "Why are *you* in my bedchamber?"

"I'm sorry," the maid said choking. "They… they threatened me, they did, your brother and the other." She sent a furtive glance to the cup on the bedside table.

"Or bribed her more like." Edme bent over the empty cup, sniffing. "Ye drugged your mistress's chocolate. *Ach*, and Hatherot drank it, the drunken fool."

Lady Ottilia's eyes flashed. "You took a bribe to drug me?" She lifted her hand, and when the girl flinched, dropped her fist back to her side. "How could you, Birdie? Who bribed you? What did they plan to do—"

"That's enough." Herbert snatched Lady Ottilia and tossed her over his shoulder. "I'll tie you to his bed, and it will work just as well."

While Lady Ottilia squirmed and beat on his head, Edme blocked the door. "Whose bed?"

"His lordship's," Birdie said, sobbing.

Edme's mind swirled... his lordship...

Cottingwith. They'd planned to compromise him into marrying Lady Ottilia.

Anger surged sending her heartbeat into a wild tattoo. She oughtn't to have trusted the woman... except, Lady Ottilia's alarm was genuine. She wanted Sir Henry, not Trent.

"Stop that." Herbert slapped the only reachable part of Lady Ottilia, her bottom. She kicked harder and shrieked, an earsplitting scream that would get everyone in the house out of bed.

"I won't do it," the maid wailed. "I won't strip her. I won't have any more part of this."

Herbert freed a hand and slapped the maid who fell back. Her head hit the bedside table with a crack, and she slid to the floor again, her eyes fluttering shut.

"You," he said to Edme, "I'm locking you in. The marquess will wake soon enough. I'll strip her ladyship myself."

"Like hell you will." Lady Ottilia writhed, kicked, pounded, and reached behind to claw at his head and face. Swearing, he cast her down. She hit the bed and slipped to the floor.

Edme saw it all in slow motion: Lady Ottilia scrambling; Herbert's fist poised to hit her.

The poker lashed out and struck with a sickening crack. Eyes wide, Herbert lunged for Edme. She dodged him, hit him again, and he fell to the floor.

Blood poured from the side of his head.

Stomach tumbling, Edme lurched to the wall, trembling and unsteady, only dimly aware that someone was pounding, that Lady Ottilia was scrambling to her feet. The lamp in the room sputtered again. Edme staggered against a bureau, her legs suddenly too weak to hold her.

Strong arms came around her, and she jerked trying to pull away.

"It's me, my love."

Cottingwith. Cottingwith was here.

"She's fainting," another male voice said.

"I'm not. I never—"

"Shhh."

Cottingwith bent close, and her feet left the floor.

149

She closed her eyes, drew in the scents of shaving soap and horse, and heard the murmur of voices in the crowded room.

"Aye, it's true. M'sister never faints. Is Hatherot dead?"

"See to this." Trent's voice rumbled in her ear. "Jelson, that's Taylor's nephew. Take him."

"Sir Henry." Lady Ottilia choked. "He was going to… to force me…"

The lady's voice trailed off in a rush of cold air as Trent carried her into the passage.

"What has happened? What has this girl done to Lady Ottilia?"

Edme tightened her grip on his shoulder. Trent's mother was here.

"Go to your room, Mother," he said sternly.

"I told you not to invite—"

"To your room," he said in a tone Edme hoped she'd never hear directed at herself.

The voices trailed off and they followed a bobbing lamp to the end of the wing and stopped in front of a door. Mrs. Hunnycrest paused and glanced back.

"The screams woke some of the guests and servants. I'd best get them back to bed," she said, and disappeared.

Edme touched her rescuer's cheek. Scratchy. "Where are we?"

"My bedchamber." He opened the door.

Her brain began to clear. "Herbert was taking Lady Ottilia here. He meant to... to take off her clothes and put her into your bed. He meant to compromise ye." She thought about the awful crack of the iron against the footman's head... "Where's my poker?"

"Archie disarmed you."

Ah. She could barely remember her brother's presence.

"What would possess your footman to try to do that to Lady Ottilia?"

"It was probably Hatherot's idea."

"Or your mother's," she mumbled and suddenly lifted her head, her heart pounding. "Did I kill him?"

He shushed her again, set her tenderly on the bed, and went to fetch drinks. Edme stood and moved to a chair.

Cottingwith paused, smiling, and handed the glass into her shaking hands.

"Good Kinmarty whisky for my Scottish hoyden," he said. "Drink it down."

She took a sip and closed her eyes, letting the liquid burn through her.

When she opened her eyes, Cottingwith was on his knees before her.

* * *

COLOR FLOODED EDME'S CHEEKS. SHE WAS SHAKY still, her topaz eyes wide and bright, and so beautiful that his heart leaped in his chest. His duties this night weren't finished. Taylor had to be found; Mother needed to be subdued; and Hatherot... damn the troublesome man, if he could put him too on that ship at the Nore, he'd do it.

Those troubles could wait for a few moments.

He took the glass and set it aside, then lifted Edme's hand and kissed the chilly palm. "I've never been so frightened in all my life, seeing you standing there with that poker and two bodies on the floor."

"Did ye th-think I'd hit ye as well?"

He hugged her and laughed, and she joined in giggling, the most beautiful girl in the world. His golden goddess, a strong girl who could joke after such a terrible danger.

Before he could kiss her, a frown formed a line between her brows. "Did ye find Taylor?"

"Not yet. We're searching the house." And he would go and join that search in a minute.

A distant scream rent the night and frantic pounding interrupted them. Mrs. Hunnycrest burst in.

"My lord." She huffed out the words. "Taylor. Coming down from the nursery. The others have gone downstairs already."

His heart lurched and he leapt to his feet. "Sally—"

"She's not there." Edme stood. "Nor the duke's bairn. They're both in my bed."

His brilliant lady. He dropped a quick kiss on her lips. "Stay here. Lock the door." And then he hurried behind the beckoning housekeeper.

"Wait." Edme clutched his arm and tried to hand him a fireplace poker. He shook his head and showed her the pistol he'd carried that evening. "You keep that."

Stomping feet and another woman's scream came from the upper floor.

He squeezed Edme's hand. "Hunnycrest, go. Fetch help."

Then he ran to the landing, silk whispering behind him.

Edme had joined the pursuit. His Scottish hoyden. He'd have to protect her too.

A figure in white bobbed and swayed down the stairs from the nursery. He and Edme pressed back against the wall, and a man dressed in black materialized next to a woman in a nightdress.

Not one of his servants. He supposed it was Kinmarty's child's Scottish nursemaid.

Edme gasped. He placed a finger over her lips and shook his head. Though a dim lamp glowed in the passage, Taylor hadn't seen them yet.

The lamp caught a glint of metal, and Trent's nerves thrummed. Taylor held a knife poised at the maid's neck while his other hand clutched the young woman's middle.

It had been years since he'd fired at an enemy's head, and it was damnably dark. Still, if the maid would move out of the way just enough, a clean shot would solve the problem of his mother.

The maid's eyes flashed as she twisted her head away from the knife at her throat. "Ye're hurtin' me, ye mawworm."

She'd seen them, but Taylor hadn't.

As Trent raised his pistol, a door in the passage beyond opened and two heads popped out. On the other side of the corridor, the duchess poked her head out too.

The blasted Darnley girls and the blasted duchess. That was Edme's suite, and the children were there as well.

There were more footsteps behind them. He couldn't risk a bullet ricocheting.

Trent stowed his gun and stepped out of the shadows. "Let the maid go, Taylor. Your quarrel is with me."

Behind him, Edme muttered something. The maid spun aside, and Taylor flew at him, knife poised.

HEART POUNDING, EDME PRESSED AGAINST THE WALL. Morag, the maid, fell back. Joanie rushed out, swept an arm about Morag, and tugged her through the doorway.

In the corridor, Trent parried a knife thrust and landed a sickening crunch with his left fist.

The reserved earl fought like a savage.

But Taylor was just as wild, older, but strong, and desperately trying to dodge the hangman's noose.

If she could just get close with her poker. *Ach*, but she might hit Trent instead.

Her heart twisted and squeezed as the fight went back and forth, Taylor slashing, Trent dodging and rolling. With one flurry of punches, Trent had the villain against the wall squeezing his knife hand. With a roar, the butler broke free and slashed.

Sleeve torn, Trent feinted, ducked, and tripped backward, trying to scramble to his feet.

Gasping for breath, Taylor stood over him, wild-eyed.

Before she could raise the poker, Edme was shoved aside.

"Don't do it, Taylor. Don't hurt my son."

Mrs. Yardley's bulk filled the space, even as her voice shook. The duke had a grip on her arm, holding her back from rushing the butler.

Still, the lady teetered closer, tugging at Taylor's attention, drawing the point of the knife toward herself.

Taylor turned a glassy-eyed gaze on her, and his lips curled in a sneer.

"The son you call a fool behind his back, madam?"

Edme could hear the woman's breaths wheezing like a fireplace bellows.

"It's me who's the fool, putting trust in you."

Edme edged along the wall. Trent's mother had gone a pale shade of gray. The duke wasn't pulling her back—he was holding her up.

From the edge of her vision, she saw Trent rise. In a flash, he'd pressed his gun to the villain's ear, and it clicked as he cocked it.

"The knife," Trent said, in a genial tone. "Drop it."

"Or what? You'll splash my brains over the walls in front your mother and all of your guests?"

The corridors had filled with onlookers in night clothes.

"Yes. That's correct."

The cold tone sent a chill through her. Now that he had a clear shot with naught but a wall behind Taylor—a thick one, she hoped—Trent wouldn't waver. Her English earl was no milksop, no weak passionless English nobleman.

Taylor sniggered, and the knife clattered to the floor. A man rushed forward to retrieve it, another pushed past Mrs. Yardley as Trent stowed his gun.

"Aye," Taylor said, laughing again. "Take me if you

156

will, but I'll warrant I won't even stand trial, not with the evidence I can offer against your m—"

Crunch. Taylor crashed to the side, smacked into a wall sconce, and thudded to the floor.

Mrs. Yardley swayed into the duke's arms.

"Help my mother to her room," Trent called. "And fetch the doctor."

While the housekeeper marshalled the servants and led Mrs. Yardley off, a sandy-haired man hurried over.

"Just like the old days, Yardley," he said. "Grim business in your own home, though."

Edme pushed past the man and snatched up Trent's arm. "Dear God…" She swallowed sudden moisture.

His arms came around her. "Edme love, this is my old shipmate, Thomas Jelson."

She sniffed and nodded. "Pleased to meet ye. Why are ye here? We were planning to visit ye."

"He's come down from Chatham to help us."

She nodded. With Trent's mother being implicated, she supposed there were few local people he could call on to help.

"Tom, meet Edme Beecham, Archie's sister. My fiancée." His gaze held hers, flashing uncertainty. "Unless…"

Oh. The change in topic rendered her dizzy.

She drew in a breath. He'd almost been killed.

She'd almost lost him, and the thought was unbearable.

She loved the man.

"Aye, Trent. I'll marry ye."

He beamed one of his rare smiles and pressed his lips to hers. The reserved earl again, his kiss was gentle and brief.

"Let's finish up here and go back to my bedchamber," he said.

Jelson chuckled. "I wish you both happy. My Rose will be pleased to meet you. For now, Yardley, I'll take care of your two miscreants. None the wiser." He winked. "Sir Henry is busy with his lady."

Jelson went to help bind Taylor and get him to his feet.

Archie joined them. "Ye'll be happy to know the footman's not dead, Edme. Glad ye found Taylor. I missed the first part of your fight, but I'm glad ye bested him."

* * *

TRENT WAS HOLDING HIMSELF TOGETHER BY A thread. It had been a near thing, and without Mother's intervention... Why had she done it? He shook his head. He'd have to ponder that later.

He felt a tug on his sleeve and looked down into Edme's burning eyes. She'd had her own near thing this night, and it showed.

"Let's go have a look at your hand," she said. "Archie, tell Mrs. Hunnycrest to let us know when the doctor arrives."

Jelson had Taylor. Sir Henry would leave with Lady Ottilia. Hatherot—he'd sleep through the night, if not longer. And Mother...

That tug again. "Your bedchamber, Trent," Edme said.

"I'm not going to want to be interrupted."

Color bloomed on her cheeks, but rather than back away, she set off toward his bedchamber, tugging his arm.

"Where are ye going?" Archie asked. "Your rooms are that way, Edme, and I understand there's a crowd there."

"Gooseberries, all of them," Edme said. "We don't need chaperones."

Trent waved Archie away. "Edme and I are going to be married."

"By special license," Archie called.

He looked over his shoulder and saw Archie's grin.

Heart hammering, he ushered her through the door and locked it. When he turned, she flew into his arms.

"Kiss me," she said, and her lips pressed against his, her arms circled his neck, her hands raked the back of his head.

Hot desire swept through him, more than just

battle lust, and her passion matched his. Her skirts came up, her legs wrapped around him. He scooped her up by her bottom, carried her to the bed and set her down gently.

She fell back and brought him down atop her.

Angling his head, he found her lips, and the kiss lit a fire in him. He rocked against her, his privy counsellor straining to break free, pushed under her skirt and slid a hand past her garter, up her bare leg, rejoicing she hadn't adopted the fashion of wearing pantalettes.

When he reached the soft silk between her legs and feathered a touch there, she gasped.

He lifted his head. "Too fast?"

"I..."

Dainty fingers swept over his cheek. Ye've quite the whiskers." She blinked and a tear trickled down. "I thought I might lose ye."

"Oh, my darling. Don't cry. I'm here."

"Did ye fight like that in the navy."

"Sometimes. On a boarding party or two."

"I was wrong about ye. I thought ye were... were..."

"Cold."

"Archie told ye."

"Yes."

"A cold Englishman. Kind, 'tis true, until ye left me last Christmas."

He opened his mouth, but she set her finger to silence him.

"I understand now. If ye truly want me, I won't be a placid wife. I want kisses, and this, and children. I won't be ignored, and I won't share ye with mistresses. It might be the English way, but I won't do it."

"Agreed. Nor will I share you with lovers."

"Then yes, I'll marry ye." She chewed her lip. "Oh, but what are we to do about your mother?"

He winced.

"And your hand." She tried to struggle up. "I forgot—"

"It's fine. But you're right. Mother needs to be dealt with. I'm going to move her to the dower house, if that's agreeable to you. Sally will live here."

"Oh dear. I forgot about Sally."

He rolled away and stared up at the canopy. Her gown rustled as she faced him. She was wearing entirely too many garments, and he wouldn't likely have a chance to get them off her this night. And probably shouldn't even try.

He heard the dreaded scratching at the door—that would be his valet, roused from his sleep—and glanced at her. She was smiling.

"I promise ye, Trenton Yardley, I won't mention either of them in our marriage bed."

"Because you'll be too distracted to even think of them."

Her hand cradled his cheek. "I want ye too."

The scratching had turned to knocking, but desire surged in him, drowning out the noise. Devil take it—they could all wait.

"Come here," he said, and pulled her into his arms.

* * *

GIVEN THE EVENTS OF THE PREVIOUS NIGHT, TRENT expected a more subdued Christmas than Trent's mother had planned for. Yet, with Taylor and his nephew having vanished, and Mother confined to her bed on doctor's orders, it was altogether a more joyful one.

He'd visited his mother more than once, only to find her asleep—or feigning sleep.

Under Edme's management, the children's Christmas Eve party was boisterous. And at the formal dinner Christmas Eve night, guests greeted the official announcement of his and Edme's engagement with warm congratulations.

As it turned out, Lord and Lady Darnley had slept through the drama, as had their sons, who'd passed out from drink in the billiards room. Their two jolly daughters chided their brothers mercilessly for missing out on the fun, and then threw themselves into entertaining the children that morning, especially Sally.

Hatherot, however, had remained abed in his sister's room unable to attend any of the festivities. The strong dose of laudanum Taylor prepared for Lady Ottilia might well have killed the lady if she'd taken it as they planned.

She hadn't returned to Furningwood for the holiday dinner. By the time Hatherot caught up with her, she'd be Lady Rylston.

After a light supper on Christmas night, Trent bid his guests farewell. The Darnleys were traveling on to their home, and the Kinmartys were anxious to return to London and spend time with the duke's nephews. They'd all leave early the next morning, even Hatherot.

All except the Beechams, who were no longer truly guests. Archie had agreed to come work for Trent, and Edme in a day or two, as soon as he could make it happen, would be Lady Cottingwith.

The three of them would leave Furningwood right after the Boxing Day party, first to travel to London, and then to the ship works.

When the drawing room door finally closed on Archie, Edme gazed up at him, frowning.

"What's amiss?"

"It's Sally. Trent, might she come with us to London? Mrs. Ewell went to visit family and doesn't plan to return. Joanie said she'd stay with Sally here, but I'm not sure I entirely trust that we have weeded out all the free trading troublemakers. And...

leaving Sally behind, well, your mother will still be here."

"That's Sally and my mother in one sentence."

She lifted her chin. "We're not in the marriage bed."

"I have workers readying the dower house for Mother, once the doctor clears her to be up. And Sally will come with us."

He stroked her plump lips and watched her eyes darken. "Would that we were in Scotland. We'd already be married."

"Oh." A smile curved her lips. "Aye." She stood and reached for his hand. "Well, that's Sally settled. And your mother. I won't mention them again for the rest of the night."

EPILOGUE

SUMMER, 1825

*E*dme stood on the wooden deck and waved to the crowd on shore. Trent had declared a holiday and laborers from the ship works, the brick works, and the manor staff came down for the maiden launch of the Edme Rose, a steel-hulled paddle steamer.

Rose Jelson leaned past her husband. "I've finally forgiven you for taking first place on the name," Rose teased. "Oh, isn't it grand. Our men have done well."

Trent's arm circled Edme's back. "We had the right partners backing us."

Edme grinned up at him.

On the other side of Trent, Sally jumped and waved. "There's Joanie with Andrew."

Their baby boy, Andrew, wouldn't remember this day. But she would never forget it.

The End

A NOTE FROM THE AUTHOR

I hope you've enjoyed Edme's and Trent's story, Book Five in the Upstart Christmas Brides stories.

Many thanks go to my friends at the Bluestocking Belles, early readers of this book, and to my editor, Jude Knight.

For now, I have no plans for a Book Six in this series, but look for some of the series characters to reappear in my upcoming book, A Wallflower's Midsummer Night's Caper. Release day is June 11, 2024, but you can pre-order today. One of the Lovelace clan from Book Three, The Impetuous Heiress, is the wallflower heroine of this new tale, set on revenge against a new duke.

Reviews are the heart and soul of marketing for indie authors. If you're so inclined, I would much appreciate you taking the time to leave a review at

Goodreads, Bookbub, or the eBook seller of your choice.

To find out more about my books, visit my website at https://alinakfield.com. Sign up for my newsletter there to get a free story available only to subscribers. I won't mind if you unsubscribe after, but I'd love to have you stick around.

Happy reading!

Alina K. Field

BOOKS BY ALINA K. FIELD

SONS OF THE SPY LORD SERIES

MARRYING MR. GIBSON

Previously titled *The Bastard's Iberian Bride*

Paulette Heardwyn rushes to visit her dying guardian, set on learning the truth about her father. But the only man with answers takes his secrets to the grave, leaving her penniless—unless she marries his illegitimate son.

https://alinakfield.com/book/marrying-mr-gibson/

THE VISCOUNT'S SEDUCTION

Lady Sirena Hollister has lost everything, even her fey abilities. But when the fairies hand her a chance at a London Season, her schemes for revenge stir up an unknown enemy, and spark danger of a different sort, in the person of a handsome Viscount.

https://alinakfield.com/book/the-viscounts-seduction/

THE ROGUE'S LAST SCANDAL

Falling—literally—into the arms of the *ton*'s most

outrageous rogue seems a risky path of escape, but Maria Graciela Kingsley y Romero has no other choice. Only England's greatest spy lord can help her, and he is not to be found—so his son will have to do!

https://alinakfield.com/book/rogues-last-scandal/

THE COUNTERFEIT LADY

Vowing she'll never submit to an arranged marriage, an earl's daughter bolts for the seaside cottage that will someday be hers. But she finds her quiet refuge occupied by the last man she ever wants to see—an American artist, who's also a thief. And quite possibly one of her father's spies.

https://alinakfield.com/book/the-counterfeit-lady/

AVENGING THE EARL'S LADY

The long war is over, but honor requires vanquishing one last enemy, and the Earl of Shaldon has no time for romance. But when the lady he longs for interferes in his plot, and his enemy strikes at her, nothing else matters but avenging his lady.

https://alinakfield.com/book/avenging-the-earls-lady/

NOVELLAS AND HOLIDAY STORIES: THE MARQUESS AND THE MIDWIFE

Finalist, 2016 National Reader's Choice Award

Uncovering a lie drives a new marquess back from a self-imposed exile at Christmas to find the only woman he's ever loved. Finding her turns out to be easy, uncovering her stunning secrets, a bit harder. But winning her back will be the greatest challenge of all.

https://alinakfield.com/book/the-marquess-and-the-midwife/

A LEAP INTO LOVE

Can a gentleman be too charming?

The ladies of Upper Upton think so.

When the single ladies of the village conspire to teach their charmer a lesson that might bankrupt him, the town's loveliest young widow—who's sworn off marriage forever—steps up to warn him.

https://alinakfield.com/book/a-leap-into-love/

LILIANA'S LETTER: FINALIST, 2015 NATIONAL READER'S CHOICE AWARD

The Matchmaker Meets the Matchbreaker

Liliana Ashford's future as a professional chaperone depends on her wealthy charge's successful marriage, but her own close encounter with a scoundrel years ago makes her determined to save the girl from the same kind of rogue.

https://alinakfield.com/book/lilianas-letter/

THE GHOST OF DEPFORD HALL

A sweet Halloween short story

It's her mother's last All Hallows' Eve.

When family, friends, and tenants gather, goblins, ghouls, and ghosts are banned from this All Hallows' Eve party.

Only, no one told the Ghost of Depford Hall!

https://alinakfield.com/book/ghost-depford-hall/

COURTED BY THE EARL

Previously titled Bella's Band

A 2015 RONE Award Finalist

Saddled with his brother's title and debts, nothing about this new life makes the Earl of Hackwell want to stay— until he meets a lady with a secret that can change everything.

https://alinakfield.com/book/courted-by-the-earl/

ROSALYN'S RING: 2014 BOOK BUYER'S BEST WINNER, NOVELLA CATEGORY

Done with grieving her losses, a late nobleman's daughter has fallen into a tidy spinster's life in London. But when one snowy Christmas Eve, a young woman needs rescue, she seizes the chance to do good—and to recover a family heirloom that ought to be hers.

https://alinakfield.com/book/rosalyns-ring/

HAUNTING MISS FENWICK

Thrilled to finally have a permanent home, a Squire's daughter won't let a supernatural creature scare her away. While hunting the ghost she doesn't believe in, she stumbles upon a mysterious flesh and blood man who might be the key to all of her problems.

https://alinakfield.com/book/haunting-miss-fenwick/

LADY TWISDEN'S PICTURE PERFECT MATCH

Promised York's marriage mart and the hospitality of his cousin's doddering stepmother, Major August Kellborn is shocked to find that his fetching hostess is the one woman who stirs his heart.

https://alinakfield.com/book/lady-twisdens-picture-perfect-match/

FLOWERS FOR HIS LADY

Eleanor Gurnwood has only one goal in sight: to make this year's Christmas service beautiful for the parishioners of St. Tancred's—until the Christmas eve when a man from her past rides in on a white horse.

https://alinakfield.com/book/flowers-for-his-lady/

THE UPSTART CHRISTMAS BRIDES SERIES

THE DUKE SHE DESPISED

Hiding her true identity, a young vicar's widow takes a position as housekeeper in a remote Scottish castle at Christmas for a new duke who years ago sabotaged her chance for happiness. She quickly falls for the duke's charming but not very competent factor, not knowing that he's hiding something also—he's the duke she despised!

https://alinakfield.com/book/the-duke-she-despised/

CONVINCING THE COUNTESS

A penniless widowed countess with trade in her blood descends upon the country manor of her sons' negligent guardian, intent on confronting him about her boys' futures. Instead, she finds his younger brother, a business-minded aristocrat with a penchant for widows and a distaste for emotional entanglements. A man who once witnessed her greatest humiliation. A man offering enticing distractions that threaten to derail all her plans.

https://alinakfield.com/book/convincing-the-countess/

THE IMPETUOUS HEIRESS

Before dashing Lord Loughton can make amends with his neglected fiancée, the lady's meddling cousin delivers her to his doorstep. He soon realizes more is amiss than his carelessness. Can he uncover her secrets and win her back before he loses her altogether?

https://alinakfield.com/book/the-impetuous-heiress/

THE NABOB'S DESIGNING DAUGHTER

Ripped from his prestigious London practice to deliver a Highland duke's heir, a young doctor finds there are more snares awaiting than a risky birth, including a surprise—and worthless—bequest. There's also his best friend's cousin, who's blossomed from mousey to heart-stirringly beautiful, with enough wiles to convince an ambitious man that his heart belongs in the Highlands.

https://alinakfield.com/book/the-nabobs-designing-daughter/

THE MACBETH SERIES

FATED HEARTS

A Love After All Retelling of the Scottish Play

A Scottish Baron returning from two decades at war meets the wife he divorced and the daughter he disavowed before she was born, only to learn that everything he'd believed was a lie. Determined to win back the only woman he's ever loved he must first face the viper who drove them apart.

https://alinakfield.com/book/fated-hearts/

THE COMTESSE OF MIDNIGHT

A Scottish Earl on a quest for the elusive Comtesse de Fontenay, rescues a French lady smuggler during a devastating storm, taking shelter with her. As the stormy night drags on, he suspects she knows the lady he's seeking, the lady who holds the secret to his identity.

https://alinakfield.com/book/the-comtesse-of-midnight/

CLAIMS OF THE HEART

Since a perilous fall, Lucie Macbeth has been seeing more than a settled future as the heiress to a Scottish barony. The visions plaguing her include a man—one far above her class and breeding, and English to boot. He's engaged to a duke's granddaughter as well, and thus wholly inappropriate. Though she can't marry him, and she won't become any man's leman, when the Sight warns her of danger to him, her conscience, and her heart tell her she can't walk away.

https://alinakfield.com/book/claims-of-the-heart/

UNDER THE HARVEST MOON

A Bluestocking Belles Collection with Friends

As the village of Reabridge in Cheshire prepares for the first Harvest Festival following Waterloo, families are overjoyed to welcome back their loved ones from the war. This collection of nine engaging tales has mysteries, secrets, tensions, reunions, romance, and makes for an unforgettable read.

Includes *Under the Champagne Moon*,

by Alina K. Field.

https://alinakfield.com/book/under-the-harvest-moon/

COMING DECEMBER 26, 2024

CHRISTMASTIDE KISSES

A Bluestocking Belles Collection with Friends

Six stories of love and romance at Christmas, includes

Twelfth Night Treasure, by Alina K. Field, a short, sweet sequel to *Flowers for his Lady*

COMING JUNE 11, 2024:

A WALLFLOWER'S MIDSUMMER NIGHT'S CAPER

Book 15 in The Revenge of the Wallflowers multi-author collection.

A Midsummer Night's masquerade at her family's country home presents the Honorable Nancy Lovelace with the perfect opportunity for revenge against the man who ruined her first London season—a man she's known since childhood, a man she once thought she loved.

https://alinakfield.com/book/a-wallflowers-midsummer-nights-caper/